Murder on the Goderich Local

Don Hayward

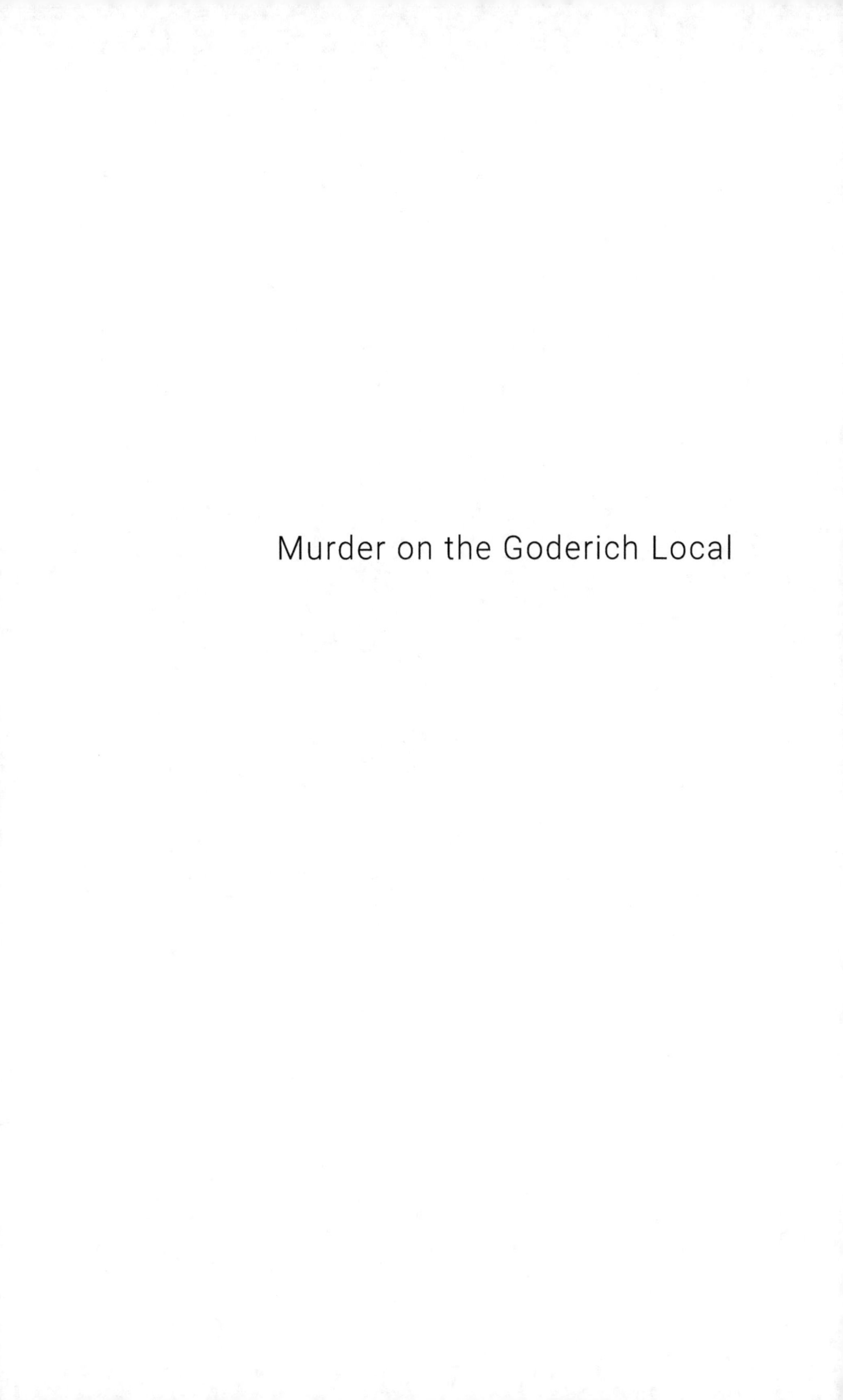

Murder on the Goderich Local

CONTENTS

Murder on the Goderich Local

A Mike Donovan Mystery

By Don Hayward

Also by Don Hayward

Collapse
Book One of After the Last Day
ISBN 978-1-7752459-2-6 (Soft cover)

Under Shadows
Book Two of After the last Day
ISBN 978-1-7752459-4-0 (Softcover)

The End of Shadows
Book Three of After the Last Day
ISBN 978-1-7752459-5-7 (Soft cover)

The Seventh Path
ISBN 978-1-62137-949-2 (Soft cover)

Journey's End
ISBN 978-1775-245933 (Soft cover)

Murder on the Goderich Local
ISBN 978-1-62137-993-5 (Soft cover)

Sherwood Green
ISBN 978-1-7752459-0-2 (Soft cover)

Return
ISBN 978-1-7752459-7-1 (Soft cover)

RoH —Alien Legacy
ISBN: 978-1-7752459-8-8 (Softcover)

Echo of the Whip-poor-will
ISBN 978-1-7752459-1-9 (Soft cover)

High Falls
A pictorial history

ISBN 978-1-7752459-6-4 (Soft cover)

All of Don's books, except High Falls, are available in an electronic version from Smashwords.com and Amazon (and soft cover on Amazon).

Most books are available through book sellers worldwide.

Contact Don,

haywardon@gmail.com

Dedicated to Chuck Ramsey, the honorary coach for our midget house-league hockey team in 1962-63 Espanola Ontario, a man I should have known better.

And my friend, Merilyn Quesnel, now passed on, who inspired me to keep writing through her wit, insight, and joy for the written word.

They both live in my memory.

Acknowledgement

I would like to thank all the mystery writers who provided such wonderful entertainment through the years.

To Mr. Lammi, who let us ride in the back of his Willy's Jeep pickup truck to meet the steam-powered mail train in the 1950s.

To my father, who took me on my first train ride and for wonderful visits on the Alliston station platform watching the big six wheeled locomotives. It's where my love of rail began.

As always, my wife Diane has spent many patient hours editing, giving wise advice and making the work more readable.

Chapter One

In the bright morning sun, the wheel-polished rails of the Canadian Southern Railway formed silver wires running through the countryside, tying Goderich to Guelph. When it emerged from the arched tunnel at Blyth, the steel formed a long shining arrow, pointing east, straight, and true, until the disrupted hills and swales of the Conestogo and Grand Rivers sent them in curving arcs to Elmira.

The track ran through cuts and over fills, beneath stately white elm trees, past maple bush, ripening fields of wheat and barley, and pastures occupied by contented Holstein milk cows and Hereford beef cattle. Occasionally, a farmer wandered through a hayfield, wondering when he could make his second cut of fodder. In the winter, this would be a snowy wasteland with frequent massive drifts off Lake Huron blocking the dead-straight track.

The men who ran the trains were not too unlike the track itself, but they more resembled the twists and turns of the rougher parts, seeking the easier way but still true to their purpose. In parallel to the tracks, they had their share of bumps, diversions and outright wrecks. Still, the men laboured on, the old ones with steam, heat, cold, soot and sulphur in their faces, their working days spent inches and seconds from burning, scalding disaster.

The younger ones running the belching smoother diesels showed more of the cockiness that comes from the reliable instant response of the machines to button push and lever movement. Both types were married to their locomotives, but perhaps in contrast to the cranky, stubborn, unforgiving steamers, the internal combustion inventions demanded less love.

On this late July morning, train 111, a mixed-freight manifest rolled across Highway Four at Blythe, eased at yard-speed through the town and ran under the arched bridge of the long abandoned Grand Trunk Line. The engineer always eased off on the throttle there, coasting the locomotive through the tunnel to keep the crew from being choked by boiler smoke. A big Pacific steam locomotive emerged from the arched tunnel, bellowing black smoke and puffing loudly as it struggled to get to line speed. The green light above the two red signals gave the clear-to-go to high speed.

For the Pacific locomotive 1232, this meant fifty miles per hour. The fireman laboured to charge coal into the demanding inferno of the boiler's firebox. Country roads crossed the track almost every mile or two. The train whistle sounded frequently, two shorts, a long, a short and a lingering long wail as the engine cleared the roadways. Sulphurous black and white smoke and steam bellowed from the stack, drifting over the countryside, tracing the progress of the freight train.

That could have been my life, thought Walter Edwards as he waved from the fireman's window at a farmer riding an old Massy-Harris 'share-cropper' as he inspected the railway fence along the south side of his pasture. Years ago, Walter had dreamed of having a farm, before reality forced him onto the railway.

The farmer waved back in envy.

That could have been me, he remembered, *if father hadn't gotten sick, leaving me to take over the place, damned war.*

He impatiently pushed the tractor's hand feed throttle. Black smoke bellowed from the rusty muffler sticking up from the fading red engine hood.

Walter Edwards threw a shovel-full of coal deep into the firebox. Al hit the throttle and black smoke puffed angrily from the G5 Pacific stack as it powered up an incline.

At Mile 49, the throttle came off, and the train slowed, squealing from brakes being applied intermittently with the whistle howling through the crossing at Highway 23. Before the Mile 47 marker, the locomotive eased through the switch on the west end of a siding that allowed cattle cars to be set for loading. This side track only allowed enough room for a dozen freight cars. The train squealed to a stop before the second switch at the east end of the siding. A white cloud blew sideways, blasting loudly above the track ballast as the cylinders cleared.

"Get that damned car uncoupled," Albert O'Connell gave Bobby Ellis a shove.

The brakeman went down the ladder face first, lugging a big wrench which he threw towards the switch stand. The switch usually stuck because of infrequent use. Bobbie hated this drop and hurried to the second boxcar behind the engine tender, looking over his shoulder, expecting to see provincial cops rushing from the bush.

He yanked the coupling-pin bar and waved. The locomotive lurched forward, drawing the remaining car as the airline connector snapped apart, hissing and dropping stiffly towards the track. Bobby hurried to unlock the switch arm, yanking on the operating handle and whacking it hard with the wrench to free the reluctant mechanism. The big steam locomotive backed the boxcar into the siding with Bobby riding the fore ladder, searching the trees for a Provincial Police greeting party. They squealed to a stop opposite a gate beside the empty stock pens. He quickly set the brake, uncoupled the boxcar and rode the tender back to the switch. In a few minutes, the train, less boxcar 315387, was ready to roll.

Al threw the throttle forward impatiently. They were always behind schedule after this drop. He shared Bobby's nervousness. The six big drive-wheels spun a shower of sparks. Black smoke shot from the stack. The slack came off too fast, and the couplings crashed as the train stretched.

"How not to start a train," Walter tried to tease O'Connell.

"We're behind time now," Al growled back, as anxious as Bobby to be clear of the dropped boxcar.

He eased off and let the engine coax the train into motion. Bobby snagged the moving ladder and climbed into the safety of the cab, throwing the wrench ahead of him.

Al's snarly this morning, thought Walter, *but at least not hung over. He's always better when Millie has him under her wing for the night.*

Walter Edwards was Albert O'Connell's fireman. Walter and Al had worked together for over ten years, always on the Goderich sub. Years of stoking boilers had made Edwards tough physically, but he was a thoughtful man. He did not much like Al's rough edges, his bullying and his capacity for guzzling Red Caps.

Walter Edwards had no ambition to become an engineer. It would have meant more years on the spare board. He had hated being the low seniority man with irregular hours. Now, he had a stable income, augmented by the twenty-five dollar bonus from the just dropped carload, and a home life in Guelph with his wife. It was quiet now that the kids had all moved out. Retirement loomed, and he was content. The only sacrifice was lying over at Maitland Station on weeknights.

Al had lost his family long ago. The beer, the irregular hours, and his wife having found a war job in Toronto had contributed to the inevitable end. O'Connell liked the layovers in Millie's Hotel. He had his own room but usually shared Millie's bed.

Down the line to the east, the Goderich bound morning combination was waiting on a siding. Bill Blatchford felt the comforting vibrations of the RS3 diesel at idle and watched the glowing headlamp of the steam locomotive. He contemplated the growing bulk of the approaching black engine. Steamers were certainly romantic and beautiful, but they were old-fashioned. This RS was a joy, even with its paint fading and the rattles of aging sheet metal shaken loose bouncing over the uneven track bed. Bill lusted for a mainline job, running one of the newer, more powerful GP locomotives on the smooth tracks between Toronto and Windsor. There was more pay and more prestige in the mainline runs between big cities. He might even get to run pure passenger trains instead of these milk-stopping consists. Blatchford was young, ambitious, and ruthless. In his book, these branch subs were for losers.

The approaching Pacific was dirty, drafty and required more care than a diesel. Blatchford sat in his padded driver's chair in comfort. Today, the electric fan cooled him and Jones. In winter, the heater kept them snug. Starting and stopping was a simple matter of throttle and air brake. No coal to shovel, no soot in your face. The Pacific, bellowing smoke as it worked up the slight grade, roared past the impatient diesel idling on the passing track. Bill gave a toot on the horn and waved. The Pacific engineer stared back, unmoving.

Stubborn bastard, thought Blatchford.

As he approached, Albert O'Connell watched the new- fangled engine. Its headlight seemed to bully. He imagined his G-5's lamp staring back, defiantly.

"Look at that bully, leaving his headlamp on to scare us, bastard. He deserves a whack up the side of the head."

The headlamp of the diesel locomotive went out, as it should for a train waiting on the passing track. They set the switches to the main line.

"Guess you scared him good," Walter laughed at Al.

Edwards knew how far he could push O'Connell before the man's quick temper might take control. Al had a slower fuse at work. Walter once saw the people in the trainmaster's office in Guelph play Al like a fiddle, taking him to the edge of exploding and then backing off.

O'Connell would not risk fighting and losing his job, but he had his limit. His 'off time' was different. Walter had once crossed Al's temper-line in Millie's dining room. O'Connell had laid him on the floor with one punch. Walter did not want to get banned from the hotel and had not fought back. Millie seemed to blame Al and sent him upstairs as punishment.

"I'll get him good, one day," O'Connell muttered to Walter as he focused on Blatchford in the RS3. "You know I can."

As they roared past the RS3, Al heard the arrogant toot on the diesel's horn. The Pacific's drive wheels clacked over the switch frog.

The devil's horn, Albert thought, although he never went to church.

The diesel driver's wave looked like a dismissive put down. It didn't help that Albert no longer got to run passengers since Blatchford had that run. The CSR thought the smoke was too much. Diesels were cleaner. The waiting train, number 100, was the morning Goderich bound combination, comprising mixed freight trailed by an express car and a lone passenger coach.

Damn them!

"Look at that tin can," O'Connell said, nodding at the combination fast disappearing as they sped east. "They'll never last. They aren't as powerful as Georgie is. The only dash it's got is in its name." Al always wrote RS3 as RS-3.

"They are the way of the future," Bobby said. "CSR is replacing the 0-6-0 Goderich yard engine with a diesel."

"What do you know, you stupid pup?"

Bobby frowned. He had no love for Al but put up with him for this regular job on the Goderich sub. It was the young man's only way to get off the spare board. He needed the regular money. Roberta needed his help. He and Walter had more in common.

Al's kind of right, he thought, *little kids won't stay at the Goderich station for hours watching a boring diesel switcher.*

They sped on. Albert loved this old Pacific locomotive. She was a living friend, fussing and hissing, sharing his impatience. He ran his hand over the brass throttle handle worn shiny beneath his glove and looked at the windowsill where years of forearms, especially his, had polished cheap wood into fine luster. Firebox heat filled the cab, heat he cursed in August for being there and cursed in January for not being enough. This old Pacific had personality. She was his second mistress. To Albert, her name was Georgie, a wild, loving girl. She could be mean.

Sometimes, Georgie needed to be coaxed, but today's manifest was easier. Train 111 was a long line of empty grain cars with a couple of road graders on flat cars and boxcars of mixed freight. The return, 110, would have Georgie pulling her limit, a full load of grain for the ships and steel for the Federal Machine Company. Walter hustled to spread coal into the firebox, cursing every shovel full.

"I hate this effing banjo," Walter glared at his shovel. He and the coal scoop had carried on a love, hate relationship for over thirty years. CSR would not replace the Pacific with an oil fired unit on this declining branch line. Edwards frowned at the water level sight-glass and injected more water into the boiler.

"We might have to water at Elmira," Walter said. "The drop-off uses a lot." His spirits lifted when he enjoyed the morning air.

They sped along the straight towards Elmira, rattling over the diamond that allowed the CSR and the CN Stratford to Palmerston trains to cross without stopping. Walter shared Al's dislike for diesels. Edwards knew that Blatchford, running the diesel behind them, clipping along in his oil-smelling comfort, would never feel the wind or the rails like they could in this cranky girl.

Walter glanced at the brakeman. He liked Bobby, but the young man did not understand. He and Albert had spent over thirty years each in engines like Georgie. She was their life.

Bobby will end up being a diesel man for sure. He's right, diesel is the future. These beautiful Pacific engines will soon be a memory or locked up in museums. It's good Al and I will soon retire.

The pressure gauge was showing one hundred and ninety-nine. Walter slid open the cast iron doors and threw a shovel-full of coal to the back of the firebox.

Train 100 cleared the switch onto the main line and paused for the rear end brakeman riding in the coach to reset the switch. Blatchford lost no time in moving the throttle up to the fifth notch, even though still short of the next block signal. On the Goderich sub, the blocks were four miles long to save money. Traffic had declined these days. With so few trains, Blatchford thought they could control the traffic by mail. Now that the Pacific had cleared, there was no danger of meeting another train. They soon passed the 'high-clear' signal, and the RS3 leapt ahead at full speed with the throttle lever in the eighth notch.

"Why is it, George, that once a month we end up waiting for that rattletrap of an engine? He's supposed to be on the passing track instead of us. It's always every few weeks."

"Maybe they have extra eggs at month's end," George Jones chuckled. "The hotel at Maitland has good food."

"The food's great there," said Blatchford, "and so is the service. That little waitress is sexy."

"You have a weakness for waitresses," George smiled. Irene, Mrs Blatchford, had been a server.

Bill forgot about the steamer as he ran Train-100 west. As they flew past Mile 47, he saw the out-of-place freight car parked on the cattle siding. He took off his sunglasses for a better look.

Maybe it is a bad-order. Perhaps they had a hot box, he thought. *There was one there last month too... strange.*

Blatchford was curious. The only train that could drop that boxcar was 111. They seemed to do it regularly.

"George, did you get the number of the boxcar back there at 47?"

George Jones, still called 'fireman,' in the diesel locomotive to conform to union pay scales, strained to look back. "Nope, wasn't paying attention to your side. We were going too fast. Slow down and I'll get her on the way back."

"315, something," muttered Blatchford, "remind me to check. There's something funny about that car."

"It's probably a bad-order, a cripple with a hot bearing." George stared at his side of the track. "The CSR doesn't change the trucks much on these dedicated sub freight cars."

Jones and Blatchford usually worked together three times a week. Bill ran the engine every day, but he had no sentiment for the RS3. George was more romantic and nicknamed her 'Jane', pretending the RS stood for 'Russell'. He had put a pin-up of the sexy actress beside Blatchford's picture of his pretty wife. If Bill paid as much attention to

Irene Blatchford as he did to bedding other women and getting a promotion, it might change things. George hoped Bill would never change unless he disappeared completely. Jones was still a spare man, and with the rotation, he spent two days a week on the ground in Guelph. For the moment, being on the spare board satisfied him. George looked at the pictures of Jane and Bill's wife and smiled. They compared favourably, at least in looks. Jones did not know how Jane Russell was in bed. He still had a connection to Blatchford on those off days.

Chapter Two

Train 100 squealed down the hill, across the Highway 21 overpass, and eased to a stop at Meneset Station. A semaphore guarded the track to signal passenger pickup stops at the unmanned station. Occasionally, the train-orders signal banjo required the engineer to go into the station to call down to the Goderich stationmaster. Today, a passenger was getting off and there were no special orders. The locomotive paused in the sunshine before heading into the pleasant, tree-shaded section before the bridge.

Less the one rider, Bill eased locomotive 8439 up to mid-speed, fanning the brake on the long, shallow down-slope along the riverbank to the bridge. As the front bogies rounded the curve to line up with the trestle, a square yellow flag trackside warned of work ahead. He throttled down to a single notch and eased across. Two workers stood on a safety platform jutting from the bridge, hanging high above the river on the engineer's side.

The crossing had made a spectacular impression the first time Blatchford saw it, but after so many trips, Bill no longer found it interesting. In late summer, the shallow river below was languid and slimy with gravel bars visible everywhere. Occasionally, a fish would sun in a deeper pool. It was a dry summer. The August morning mist had not yet burned off. Downstream, it shrouded the break wall that protected the headworks of the deep salt mine where the river met the lake. There was no horizon line. The lake and sky beyond the salt mine's head-frame melded together in a pearl grey. The wheels raised a hollow rumble from the tarred cross-ties and the steel supporting girders. This late in the summer, birds had abandoned their nests on the inside flanges of the steel.

"Look at those fishermen up there." George leaned back so Bill could see upriver towards the highway bridge at Saltford. Fishermen stood in hip waders in the flow. The languid water only reached their knees. A few dark silhouettes trailed line and bait in flowing current, while two others snapped long spinning rods towards quiet backwaters.

"They won't get anything," Bill said. "The water's too warm and low."

"Unlike that blue heron down there in the ox-bow," George leaned out his window for a better look, "it just speared a frog."

A herring gull suddenly lifted beside the open window and squawked at no one in particular. George started and smiled. He loved the long bridge. Sun, rain, snow, sleet, fog; whenever he crossed, he thought it suspended him between earth and heaven. Sometime, he might retire here and be one of those shadows whiling away a summer morning in the river.

Bill only thought about the main line and promotion. He waved at the two track-workers as they passed. One raised a spike-hammer in salute.

I hope they don't slip, thought Bill. *They'd die for sure in the shallow water.*

The down slope eased a half-mile past the bridge below the sharp bluff of the Lake Huron shore as they entered the Goderich yard a few hundred feet from the station. Dark shadow of the high bank contrasted with the distant green-blue of the lake. The mist was lifting rapidly, revealing several sailing boats passing offshore, taking advantage of the gentle breeze and calm water.

Train 100 squealed to a stop with the coach and express car opposite the waiting-room door. A station man pulled the lever for the knuckle pin and with two short horn-blasts and a clanging bell, Bill eased forward, snapping the air coupling, heading towards the lead switch with his freight cars. Beyond the switch, on the main track dead end, a spare coach sat just short of the derail and the buffer. It was there in the unlikely event an unusual demand overflowed the one passenger coach. The last used it a month ago during the Royal Visit.

"I guess we'll end up there eventually, on some dead end." Jones was still dreaming of ending his days in the river and sunshine. Blatchford ignored him.

The RS diverted onto the lead track, away from the parked coach.

Switcher 6275, the small 0-6-0 steam-powered yard locomotive was huffing out of the shed, adding its smoke to the morning haze, ready to distribute the newly arrived cars. Bill waved at Henry, the yard switcher's engineer. He was training to run the diesel-hydraulic shunt locomotive that was supposed to be delivered before winter.

Blatchford dropped the odd ball mix of freight cars and rolled along to the 'strong-arm' roundtable. George and the yard roustabout pushed hard on the arms to swing the locomotive around so the long-hood pointed east. They then eased up to capture flat cars loaded with road graders that Henry had deposited at the upstream stub loading ramp. It was a brief diversion, backing through the eye into the grain elevator yard where two dozen empties waited to be taken up to Maitland for tomorrow's run on 111 behind the Pacific. A large lake ship, a self-unloading grain carrier, had docked beyond the elevators. Another lay anchored offshore, waiting its turn. Across the harbour a third bulk-carrier lay, low in the water, fully loaded with salt, raising steam and about to depart. Bill exchanged friendly insults with a CN engineer performing the same operation with an S3 switcher on the parallel track.

"We're making lots of work for grumpy Al," Bill laughed at George.

6275 had placed a caboose on the main, short of the station, and was busy backing the coach and baggage car through the wye, turning them around for tonight's run of train 101. Bill backed into the caboose for the hookup.

By the union rules, this little shunt run had to have a caboose with a conductor and rear brakeman. In reality, unless there was some brass about, the caboose always rode empty. The conductor and brakeman would be in Goderich somewhere, likely the beer parlour of the Hexagon Hotel. If a manager was up from Guelph, they had to make the boring trip to Maitland Station and cool their heels in Millie's Hotel beer parlour until 6839 returned late in the afternoon to retrieve combination 101 for the evening run to Guelph. In the harvest season, they might ride extra grain trains all the way to Guelph and usually saw added salt runs in October. Today, George Jones would do all the switching. The errant rear-end crew slipped him a case of beer once a month to compensate. Jenkins, the station manager, kept a blind eye. There was a standing joke among railway men that anyone in charge of a small station had to be half-blind. In the same way, train crews knew never to embarrass or compromise the stationmasters whose deliberate blindness allowed the cut corners and goofing off.

The uphill run with the empties was light work for the RS3. They arrived back at Maitland Station just after lunch. The line up of cars was too long for the lead track. Bill backed them into the two mile spur that ran up the river to an old mill. They had built a furniture factory on the far side of the track opposite the original water-powered gristmill justifying the long service-track. The CSR lifted several boxcars of product from the place each week. Al's crew always handled the freight into and out of the factory.

Bill and George left the caboose coupled behind the RS3 on the main line in front of the station. They got stamped off by Ed, the stationmaster. George headed for the bunkhouse for a few hours' rest. Bill was eager to get to Millie's hotel.

"Good day, Mr. Blatchford," Chuck Bisco limped through the doorway into the stationmaster's office. Chuck was hoping Ed would have a job for him to earn a couple of bits. Blatchford ignored the young man.

"Hi, Chuck," Ed, stayed glued to his chair behind a cluttered desk. "Would you run down to the lead switch and set it to off the main line? 110 will be here in a bit and I want it on the lead. Here's a quarter." Ed flipped a coin to Chuck, who pivoted on his good leg and caught it easily.

"Forget the running part," Blatchford finally acknowledged Bisco with a sneer, "just hobble along and earn your charity." Bill laughed. Ed winced.

Chuck's cheeks burned in humiliation. He stared at the floor. Blatchford always made fun of his handicap. Once again, Bisco cursed the careless doctor who had damaged his leg during his breach-birth. As a kid, he had hung around the ball diamond and the arena watching everyone play. They had always treated him well. Remembering these places evoked a mixture of happiness and longing. Chuck limped out, trying not to hate Blatchford.

"Hey Ed, do you know anything about a boxcar out on the siding at Mile 47?"

Ed jerked his head towards the wall, ignoring Blatchford's question. He stared at the calendar for a long minute, listening to a loose window pane rattling from the vibration of the idling diesel just along the platform.

"Bill, shut down 6839. The exhaust is coming in."

"George won't like it if we have to do a bar over," Blatchford grumbled.

"It's a warm day. You'll be okay. I used to do it all the time when I brought an RS1 in here." The man had been the first diesel engineer on the sub before this promotion.

Ed had extracted a small amount of revenge for Chuck. He didn't like Blatchford. He didn't like the question about Mile 47. Ed hoped Blatchford would not connect the boxcar at 47 with the furniture factory.

Bill stomped out. Ed watched through the crystal-clear window as Blatchford headed to Millie's Hotel. Chuck took care of cleaning the station, paid from petty cash. He kept the Maitland Station windows the cleanest on the whole CSR system.

Ed returned to reshuffling the manifests on his desk. It was boring make-work. If it wasn't for doubling as a ticket agent, preparing cattle load manifests and the furniture factory, he would have little to do. With volume dropping, they would soon do his job from Goderich, or worse, Guelph. In that case, he would likely be back in a diesel cab.

Thinking about the furniture factory reminded him of Blatchford's question.

Nasty business, he thought.

Kathleen had flaming red hair, freckles and an ample chest that strained against her tight white blouse. The flaming hair was not a warning. Kat was gentle, even a little unsure. She was Millie's daughter and at twenty years old ran the hotel until the four o'clock drinking and supper hour. Millie always showed up to keep the boozers in line and augment the serving staff.

A gruff bar manager easily handled the beer parlour. George was a large, powerful man who had served in some secret Canadian-American commando outfit in Italy and then in Korea. He never talked about the war, but all the drunks were afraid of him. Once, an oversized mill worker from Lucknow had tried to fight him in the beer parlour. George had gently deposited the unconscious fellow onto the sidewalk. It had only taken one blow. It was the only time Millie ever saw George cry. He had slumped into a chair, trembling and wiping his eyes.

"I almost killed him, Millie. At the last second, I convinced myself it was a training fight. I never want to kill again." He had said no more.

After the incident, they left Millie to referee future skirmishes while focusing on the eatery and accommodations.

Millie reserved one end of the country-elegant eatery for those who overindulged in the licensed rooms before deciding on eating. More sober clients who just wanted a meal usually filled the main room. They hid the drunks behind a half wall of polished oak that had once supported translucent glass panels reaching the ceiling. A drunken patron had demolished one of the glass panels with a thrown china mug. Millie removed the others and implemented a no mercy policy with drunken troublemakers. Now, the barrier was open to the ceiling and topped by a collection of dusty geraniums. No one argued with Millie.

"Hey, cutie!" Blatchford winked at Kat as she brought his usual coffee. He always said it. She always blushed.

The menu was a formality. As usual, he ordered the daily special. Today, it was meatloaf and mashed potatoes covered in thick dark-brown gravy that competed with creamed corn for space on the white China plate. The food was cheap and good. She brought the meal, then sat opposite Bill and sipped a Coke. Over the few months Blatchford had worked on the Goderich sub, it had become routine for Kathleen to sit with him. Things were usually slow in the afternoons.

"I hear it's beautiful up at the old mill," Blatchford smiled, trying to sound casual.

It would be nice to get the girl alone.

He glanced around to make sure Kat's mother was not watching. Millie was safely upstairs. He reached out and took her hand.

"It's quiet, and there are nice places near the river where no one bothers you. I go there to draw. Would you like to see it sometime?" Her smile suggested Kathleen would not mind being alone with Bill.

"That'd be great." Bill rubbed her hand. Kathleen did not draw away. "Is it a long walk?"

"I'll borrow a car. Can you drive?" Kathleen glanced around to make sure her mother was upstairs. She squeezed Blatchford's hand.

"I have a nice Plymouth back in Guelph. Maybe you'll get to ride in it one day."

"You could drive up on the weekends," Kat said. "We could go to the beach."

Blatchford frowned slightly and then caught himself.

"Chuck has a car, and he likes me," Kat continued, "so he'll lend it. I won't tell him why. It's an automatic, because of his leg."

"How can that cripple afford a car?" Blatchford asked. "He scavenges for nickels and dimes."

"His mother supports him," Kathleen frowned. Chuck was her friend. He did everything he could to earn extra money. Kat admired that, and the fact Chuck had been with her throughout school. His limp did not matter to her. Kathleen never thought of Chuck as a cripple.

"His mother feels guilty about his leg. She bought the car and gasses it up. Chuck's a nice guy and generous. He drives me to Goderich."

Blatchford frowned. Kat wasn't sure if it was because he would sponge off Chuck, or he resented Bisco spending time with her. She hoped Bill was jealous. Chuck was fun, always making jokes. He was like a brother.

"They're changing the schedule soon." Bill squeezed her hand harder. His intent was obvious. "I'll have an overnight stay every Tuesday. Can we drive up one afternoon?"

Kathleen blushed and smiled. Blatchford was handsome and had travelled. Not like the hick boys in this township. The interesting ones were all the guys who were in the war. They had seen a lot, but they were all old guys, almost forty.

"How old are you, Bill?" she suddenly asked.

"Thirty," Blatchford said without hesitation. It wasn't the first or the worst lie he told the girl. He was really thirty-six. Ten years' difference would be okay, but Kat might think he was an old man at his actual age. As long as he could keep Jones away from Kathleen, his bigger secret would be safe. He did not like the signals from Kathleen. She was thinking about the future. Blatchford thought of her as entertainment, a fling like most of his conquests. Bill was adept at telling women what they wanted to hear.

"Old and wise," Kat flirted.

The Pacific rolled towards Maitland Station drawing train 110 at yard speed. Al O'Connell could see the diesel and caboose blocking the main line and the switch already set to put him onto the lead.

"Look at that bastard blocking us," Al snarled.

"Six in one, half dozen in the other," muttered Walter. "We still have to do the switching and juggling no matter where we start."

"We're too long for the lead. I'm going to roll by so Milt and Jim don't have so far to walk from the caboose. Then I'm backing up beside that rat bag. Our tail will be out on the main, but that ass can worry about it later."

"Keep steam up," Al said to Walter as he dismounted under his own good head of steam. "I'll find Blatchford."

Al headed into the station. The tail end crew tagged along. They had more to do before stamping out, but it was nice to stretch their legs.

"Blatchford's over at Millie's, as usual," Ed said and changed the subject. "There are a couple of loaded boxcars up at the factory. Lift them today." The stationmaster frowned. "It's a rush order. Winslow threatened to send it all by road. Add them onto the tail of the empties."

It disgusted Al. There was no longer a shunt engine at Maitland. The 2-6-0 Mogul switcher rusted in the engine shed. The Pacific would have to do it all, adding at least an hour to Al's day. He wanted to see Millie, and he wanted to eat and get a beer.

"Hey, gimp," Al snarled at Chuck Bisco, "here's a quarter. Go get Blatchford from Millie's. Tell him he owes you two bits more," Al laughed.

O'Connell was not shy about belittling Chuck. Since he always paid the boy for errands, the engineer thought he had the right to make fun. Al could not see it from the young man's point of view. He normally never wondered what was on other people's minds.

Chuck limped out the door, wondering which of the two railway men he disliked the most. He would never ask Blatchford for money. He did not want more abuse. Al was just trying to use him to mess with Blatchford.

Chuck stopped at the dining-room door, pulled a handkerchief from the back pocket of his coveralls and mopped his brow. The minute gave him time to calm his disappointment. He could see Blatchford holding Kat's hand. Chuck knew he had no right to have expectations, but it still hurt. He limped through the dining room to Blatchford's table.

"Mr. Blatchford," Chuck did not enjoy talking to the man. "Mr. O'Connell has arrived and the grain cars are ready for you. He says you need to get moving so he can run the spur." Chuck shifted nervously. His damaged leg exaggerated the effort. He wanted to lean on a chair but would not give Blatchford the satisfaction.

Bill glanced at the wall clock. He had less than an hour to get the full cars down to Goderich and hooked to 101.

"Damn," he exclaimed, "I have to run." He squeezed Kathleen's hand and stood. "Put lunch on my bill."

Chuck had to shift painfully on his bad leg as Blatchford pushed by. The bump might have been on purpose. He could not tell.

"Your hair looks beautiful." Chuck stood nervously, wanting to run but longing to sit with Kat.

"Thank you, Chuck. How's your Mamma?" Kat could see his nervousness and knew why. She tried to keep the conversation neutral and not encourage him with false hope. He was too nice to tease. He had a special place in her heart. Because of his leg, he had little prospect of ever supporting a family. Blatchford had much more promise. He had plans to go places and that would get Kat out of Maitland Station and into the big outside world. Her mother often said, *going with your heart is good, but you need someone to take care of you.*

The support Kathleen would soon need would not be the physical kind, but warm, healing love.

Al saw Blatchford hurrying across the street. He knew time was tight for the diesel to get down to the harbour.

"Time for fun." He winked at Ed and slipped into the storeroom.

"Where's that grumpy bastard?" Blatchford glanced out the window beyond his RS3 towards the Pacific resting on the lead, still attached to the line of freight cars. Bobby was sitting in the tender's shade. Walter was leaning on one of the drive wheels, looking relaxed. Edwards had watched Blatchford rush into the station and imagined the argument.

"O'Connell!" Bill shouted. "Where the hell are you? I have to get going."

Al wandered casually from the storeroom.

"I thought you'd be here waiting, seeing as how you're in a rush and all," Al smiled. "You left the yard while on duty," accusing Blatchford of a breach, Al had committed many times.

"How's Kathleen?" Ed saw the chance to stir things up. It was a boring day. Neither of these men were his favourites.

"Were you with that sweet girl?" O'Connell flared at Blatchford. "You stay away from her, you hear?"

"She served me lunch and held my hand." Bill could not resist the extra dig at the steam engineer. Blatchford could not understand why Al was protective of the girl. Maybe it was because he was sleeping with her mother. "She doesn't like old men like you."

O'Connell took a step towards Blatchford, balling his fists. His mouth was moving, but no words came. Ed stood, afraid he had gone too far and might have to referee.

"Calm down, old man." Bill didn't want a fight, just a humiliation. "I have to get moving. Back in those cars onto the main so I can hook up."

"Back 'em yourself!" Al's face was flushed.

"I can leave them. If they have to send 6275 up to get them, it'll be you they blame for clogging up the main line and making 101 late."

"I'll get you, you bastard," Al stomped out the door, growling at Walter and Bobby to get moving as he scaled the ladder.

They backed the string onto the main track and then returned to the lead, while Blatchford backed into the loaded cars and eased forward. He had no time to arrange the Goderich caboose at the end. The 8439 pulled forward and stopped with Al's caboose at the station.

"Uncouple that car," Al ordered Bobby, "be quick about it!"

Bobby scrambled out, and once he raised the knuckle pin, he signalled Blatchford. The RS3 belched black exhaust and rattled as if about to come apart. It strained to get the heavy load moving. With the bell ringing and air horn blasting a warning at the Main Street crossing, the grain cars eased away towards Goderich.

Al steamed the Pacific onto the main, hitched the caboose and deposited it onto a stub off of the lead. Milt and Jim would sleep in it overnight. The tail end crew didn't need to make the run to the factory. Then the Pacific nosed into the empties on the spur and pushed them the two miles to the loaded boxcars at the furniture factory. They would leave the string on the spur for the night. An hour later, long after the Guelph combination had run through behind the RS3, Al backed the Pacific onto the engine shed stub, over the ash pit and left her to cool down for the night man who would clean the ash box and relight her to be steam up by five the next morning. The crew trudged off to stamp out at the station. Al hurried away to see Millie.

"Ed, come up to the hotel and have a beer with us," Walter said. "I want a bite to eat before hitting the bunkhouse."

"Me too," Bobby added, "it always seems like a short night."

Ed threw his car keys into the desk drawer and grabbed his hat. There was nothing to do now until train 100 arrived in the morning. He actually liked Walter, and this young brakeman seemed okay.

"I'm with you. Just for a quick one. The misses won't like me late for supper and it's a five-minute walk."

Walter and Bobby waited as Ed carefully locked the door and hid the key behind a loose brick on the windowsill. They went past the stationmaster's sleek '55 Buick and walked across the street to the beer parlour.

"How come you don't drive home?" asked Billy.

"The Buick belongs to the CSR, so it stays at the station. I just drive home for lunch to keep it running." Ed did not mention family trips and errands that they used the railway automobile for.

On the evening run to Guelph, Bill could finally discover the number of the boxcar at Mile 47. He wrote 315387 into his journal with the note: something's funny about this car... must look into it. The car would still be there in the morning but gone by the next evening's run of 101 when Bill would note it and write the date beside his first entry.

***

The three men spent a half-hour in the beer parlour, telling rude jokes and old, half-true stories until Ed hurried off to supper. Walter and Bobbie went to the dining room. They counted themselves sober, taking a table in the main room near Al and Millie. Millie's table was next to the divider where she could keep an ear on the drunks and an eye on the cash. The till wasn't an issue tonight. Kat was serving the dinning-room customers, and Mabel, a hard bitten local woman, took care of the cooking and serving the drunkards. Mabel was not greedy and usually made her extra money from the careless tipping and occasionally short-changing her more intoxicated customers. She would never dip into the till. Millie was always watching.

Albert had time to shower and dress in fresh clothes. Millie did his laundry. Walter and Bobby were a contrast of sooty coveralls smelling of oil and sweat. They had not washed the smudges from their faces. They did not stand out from the dusty farm boys smelling of much worse than human sweat.

"I don't like Blatchford around Kathleen," Al said to Millie. "I don't like him. He'll hurt her."

"Why do you care?" Millie sounded resentful. "It's not as if you've been a father to her."

Millie had struggled to raise her daughter on her own. She was protective, but if a nice man wanted to romance Kathleen, that would be fine.

"I care about her, Millie." Al seemed sad. "There's something fishy about Blatchford."

"I'll keep an eye on her," Millie smiled. "I won't let him hurt her. If he does, he'll have to deal with me." She stubbed her cigarette firmly into the ashtray.

"I have hurt her enough." Millie glared at O'Connell.

"She's beautiful." Bobby was listening while staring at Kathleen as she fussed behind the counter.

"You stay away from her too, you little pup," Al flared. "She's too good for you. You couldn't run an engine like Georgie or a real woman." He looked at Millie.

"What do you know about running a woman?" Millie scowled. "It seems the last ten years you've forgotten how. Your fires out and they plugged your stack."

"What are you laughing at?" Al snapped at Walter, who had broken into a big grin. "We're both over the hill. When's the last time you had a full head of steam?"

"Maybe we old women need a younger man," Millie winked at Bobby.

"What? That little piece of crap." Al stood as if he was going to give Bobby a punch. Ellis stared at his shoes, sorry Millie had drawn him into the problem of the older men's declining sexual prowess. Except for admiring her feminine charms, he had no interest in Kat. He certainly had no interest in Millie, who was almost old enough to be his mother. Women got in the way of a career. He wanted to be an engineer. As his little Scots friend in the Guelph engine shed would say, "You don't need a ball and chain. Better to rent than buy."

The little Glaswegian philosopher was a drinker and his own wife had finally booted him out the door. The only woman Bobby wanted to help was his little sister, Roberta, who needed to get away from home. Actually, his own father deserved the Scot's treatment, and for the same reason.

Millie grabbed Al's hand and pulled him back into his seat.

"Shut up, you old fool." She had loved him once, at least she thought she had loved him, but now it was more of a habit. Millie needed things to be calm. She felt guilty enough about Kathleen. Millie loved her daughter. No one, not even Al, was going to cause Kat grief.

"Blatchford had better mind his P's and q's or he'll be for it," Al said loudly, wanting to divert the discussion away from his own short-comings.

Other patrons turned expectantly towards the table. Sometimes, Al put on a pretty splendid show ending with Millie dragging him through the kitchen door, adding more to the ongoing whispers and gossip in a town with little excitement. One of the local toughs once had a fistfight with a stranger who tried to insult the boring place by saying it was so sleepy Main Street needed an alarm clock. The bloodied stranger's insult had since become a local joke.

"Cut the big talk," Millie laughed. "You couldn't hurt a fly."

"Wanna bet?" Al slurred, feeling the effects of the beer.

Millie had put up with many years of Al's blustering. One time when he caught in a brawl in the beer parlour, he had flattened against the wall, dodging flying glasses, letting the drunken farm boys duke it out. She did not believe him this time.

"I need to get away from Al," Bobby and Walter headed to the bunkhouse. "He treats me like shit. If it wasn't for ending up back on the spare board, I'd stand aside. I need the money. He reminds me of my father."

"Al's retiring next year," Walter said. "Hang in there until then. I'm going just after, but you have a future. Look to the diesels."

"That's another thing," Bobby stopped and looked worried, "that box car deal might end my future."

"I don't like it either. It seems fool-proof though. No one even knows that car exists."

"No one had better find out about it."

The men walked on in silence.

Chapter Three

Bobby had enough of Al's condescending abuse. Walter might put up with it, but Bobby was angry. Walter's comment about diesels sparked a plan that would get him off the Pacific and onto an RS3.

"Bill," Bobby approached the diesel engineer on the platform a few days later. "I'd like to learn to run your engine. Could I ride with you on this back and forth you have in the afternoon?" Bobby took off his peaked cap and twisted it shyly. He was ten years younger than Blatchford and lacked the engineer's cockiness. "I could ride down with you and drop off here when you bring 101 up on your way to Guelph."

"Why would you want to do that? What's in it for me?"

"Diesels are the future," Bobby replied. "I want off that damned soot bucket and join the future. I can't offer you anything."

Bobby gazed longingly at the RS3, idling noisily on the main. George Jones was listening.

"Hey, Bill, you've always wanted to get onto the mains, but you can't, as long as there's no one on the spare board to replace you. There's a new training course for diesel engineers in a few months. I'm going to take it, and Bobby could too. Bobby could replace me, and I could replace you."

In more ways than one, he thought, *Blatchford doesn't have a clue.*

Bill liked the idea. One of his frustrations was the resistance of steam engineers learning diesel. There was no spare board for engineers for the RS3 on the Goderich sub. This would get him ahead before the CSR finally ditched steam and everyone would wake up and want a job. There were too many senior engineers who would bump him back to a spare, even on the Goderich sub, unless he was already on a mainline GP9.

Bobby promised the rear brakeman a beer a day to ride up front with Al and Walter for the hour or two of afternoon yard work at Maitland.

O'Connell would be another matter. Once Al found out Bobby wanted to train on diesels, he would make his work day even more miserable than it already was. Bobby invented a story and was ready for Al's hostility. He had plenty of practice dodging his father's abuse.

"Why would you want to ride that claptrap? You ain't a turncoat going to diesels, are you?" It surprised O'Connell when Jim, the rear end brakeman, hopped into the cab at the Maitland end of the 110 run.

"I've met a hot chick in Goderich. This way, I get to see her for an hour or two every day. She lives right up the hill from the station." Bobby tried to sound eager. Al smirked. He remembered back when Millie had been a hot chick, too.

Funny how Millie has changed, he thought.

"Have fun," he growled, "they don't last that way long."

Everyone frowned. They all liked Millie, and they knew what Al had meant.

Bobby hurried down from the Pacific before Al made him feel bad. He scooted from the lead track to climb the rear ladder of the RS3. A short blast from the air horn and Blatchford eased the engine and the line of grain cars into motion. Bobby became a regular afternoon hitch-hiker on the RS3 to Goderich and back.

When there was a purpose, Bill could be friendly. He wanted Bobby to have a good head-start for the training course. The short run to Goderich, shunting the loads of grain and then back to Maitland fronting 101 had enough challenges to cover almost all the details Bobby would need to learn, including the steep incline over the river and running for a short time at the eighth notch bringing the consist over the flat from Meneset to Maitland Station. Bill enjoyed being a teacher. It forced him to rethink the things he had been doing by habit for many months. It would sharpen him up for when he had to train on a GP9. Bobby already knew signals, coupling and switching. Bill only needed to show him the controls and the little tricks.

"These little tricks I'm showing you make it work better, but remember, the way they teach you in the course is how you do it until you have your own cab. Don't forget."

"It's the same on the Pacific," Bobby replied. "I don't think Al could get the thing moving if he tried to do it all according to the book."

"Never ignore a signal. It could get you killed." Bill admonished Bobby for a sin he committed regularly on the sub. On the main line, it could indeed be a death sentence.

Bobby made the run with Bill and George twice a week. The things he was learning thrilled him, and he enjoyed the spectacular ride down the hill to Goderich harbour.

"Make sure you take her easy here." Blatchford slipped the throttle down to the fourth notch as the engine made the curve onto the Maitland Bridge. "I think if we were in the eighth notch, we would roll her off the curve and into the river."

"I love this bridge," said Bobby. "It's a view to die for. It was sad when we stopped running it."

"I hate it," said Blatchford. "It's a stinky river, a dinky little town and a dying run. I can't wait to get a main line assignment and don't want to be here until I retire or die like Albert will. If you get the job, you'll be here when they shut the whole sub down."

Everything became routine for two weeks, and Bobby ran the locomotive for over one complete return trip. Then the CSR affected his progress.

"There won't be any return train 101 on Tuesdays," Bill said to Bobby, raising his voice above the noise of the diesel cab. Bobby thought it was a tomb compared to the Pacific's constant sound.

"Yah, we heard," Bobby replied. "Passenger traffic is down a bit."

"A big bit," muttered George, "they decided there isn't any outbound passenger traffic Tuesdays or much inbound Wednesday mornings. We get to lie over the entire night and all day Wednesday." Bill sounded eager, thinking of Kathleen.

"Not me," said Jones, "I'll switch with Johnny. I'd rather stay in Guelph overnight."

"Like the bright lights, eh?" Bobby asked.

"Yah, something like that," George smiled, thinking of two days and a night with someone else.

***

"Hey, Little Susie," Bill Blatchford strolled into the freight office beside Guelph station. The young woman behind the counter smiled and blushed. Susan was a clerk looking after manifests and car dispersals. Bill always hoped he could get the beautiful woman into bed and teased her with the lyric to last year's hit song; however, Susan was engaged and in Guelph there was a risk Bill's wife would find out. Unlike Kathleen, Susan knew Blatchford was married. Cynics called Guelph, 'Gossip Ontario'. Despite his flirting, she did not like Blatchford.

"What do you want, Bill?"

"I have a stray car," Bill answered.

"What, someone stole your Plymouth?" She faked a concerned frown.

"No," Bill chuckled, "there's a lone boxcar bouncing around on the Goderich line. I'm curious. It's boxcar 315387."

"Hey Joe," Susan called over her shoulder towards an open door, "bring your book and give us some help."

There was a grumbling reply, and a middle-aged man with a thin moustache and thinner hair wandered out. He did not appear eager.

"Joe's the expert," she said to Bill. "I'm not allowed to touch his book," she said the last loudly and then laughed at Joe, "or anything else."

"Susie-Q, you can touch it any time you want."

Joe retrieved a large hard-bound volume from the cabinet top and plopped it on the counter in front of Bill. Dust flew. Joe coughed. He was a chain smoker and his throat was sensitive. Bill stepped back a pace.

"Susan, I thought you gals were supposed to dust the furniture and make coffee." Joe was exacting revenge.

"I'll only dust and cook for the man I marry," she snarled through another laugh, "and that ain't going to be you." She made a show of dusting her own desk.

Joe gave up. Everyone in the office got along. If they weren't teasing, they were consoling one another over some personal problem. Everyone gossiped. They all gossiped about Blatchford's womanizing.

"Women!" Joe winked at Bill. "What do you want?"

"There's a stray puppy, boxcar 315387, that turns up monthly at Mile 47. What's it about?"

"Not possible," said Joe. "Box cars don't start with a three."

"That's the number on it."

"Still not possible. Boxcars start with a one. Let's see, that number," Joe opened the book with columns of numbers and related information, "is in a series of steel ended flat beds, likely hauling pulpwood up north. This book is two years old but located 315387 on the Little Current sub."

"No record of another one with the same number?"

"Does it say CSR?"

"Yes."

"Not ours. It's a counterfeit. Better check that Yankee two-dollar bill in your wallet."

"I know what I saw," Bill was becoming agitated.

"My, my," Joe tried to make a joke, "eyesight like yours and we let you run a diesel? It's a wonder you haven't gone missing. I guess the lake at Goderich is big enough for you to see and stop before you crash into it."

"I just close my eyes and hope for the best."

Joe did not like Blatchford, but he was not being mean. He was trying to be friendly the same way his office staff behaved.

Bill boiled but caught himself. The people in Guelph who ran the CSR district were a tight-knit group. If he was to get promoted, he didn't want Joe or Susan bad-mouthing him. Blatchford did not know he already had a reputation, despite evading local women. None of that would affect a promotion unless he was bedding his potential boss' wife. He had seen the woman. There was no risk of Blatchford ever sleeping with her.

Joe pulled out a form and wrote.

"What's that?" Bill asked.

"I'll report it and see if anything comes up."

"Hold off," Bill said, a little too loudly. "Let me check more up the line; I might be wrong."

Joe shrugged and put the form away. Blatchford was sure he was right, but he did not want Joe reporting it and taking the credit.

"Thanks, Joe, but now it's a bigger mystery. I'll try to get a picture to show you."

"Remember to load the film first," Joe deadpanned.

Bill headed for the door. Joe blew a cloud of dust over Susan's counter and replaced the book. She lit a cigarette and blew a smoke ring at his office door in protest. A blue cloud poured out in answer as he lit up another Export A.

"Do you have some spare change, mister?" The little girl might be ten years old but looked underfed and a little unkempt. She carried a six quart fruit basket with two empty pop bottles in it. She smoothed her skirt and smiled up at Blatchford. Bill had just closed the office door and turned down the platform towards the passenger station.

"Why aren't you in school?" Bill stopped.

"It's summer, silly. I'm hungry. Momma doesn't have any money for food," her eyes pleaded.

Bill remembered, before the war, a little boy named Billy Blatchford begging for pennies. He had hated it when most people ignored him or swore at him. He remembered the hunger.

"Come with me," he said. "Do you like pie?"

"Honey, give my little friend here a slice of that raisin pie and a glass of milk. Wrap up one of those egg sandwiches for later."

The little girl wolfed down the food, afraid to look at the big man in the striped coveralls.

"Here," Bill said as she finished the pie and pocketed the sandwich. He handed her a five-dollar bill, a lot of money, even at railway engineer wages.

"This has a pretty picture of the Queen and a nice place up north you can visit when you're all grown up. It's a pretty blue colour like your ribbon."

The girl smiled, snatched the money and stuffed it in her pocket with the sandwich. Bill laid a dollar and twenty-five cents on the counter for the food and left a dime tip.

"Go on home now. Your Momma can buy lots of bread and milk with that."

"Thank you," she blurted out. "I like the picture of the Queen. Mommy took us to Stratford to see the Queen. She said the Queen's a rich lady and we should respect her."

The girl hurried off. Bill only paid attention to adults he had a use for. He was a soft mark for hungry kids.

***

Blatchford sat in his comfortable seat in the RS cab and watched the Maitland station office. George wasn't with him today. His alternate fireman had scurried off to the hotel for lunch and a beer. He checked his watch. Almost noon. Precisely at twelve, Ed came out the front door, walked to the side of the station and sped off in his Buick, throwing gravel wildly across the empty parking lot. He turned north, going home for lunch.

He must have an eight cylinder in that Buick. Nice, but still a damned GM.

In Blatchford's world, men would get in fistfights over their make of car.

Bill hurried across the lead and main line into Ed's office. The stationmaster had avoided Bill's questions about the stray boxcar. Blatchford thought there really was a secret to be found.

How could any car get onto O'Connell's train without Ed knowing? There has to be something going on and they're all in on it.

He searched the manifests for the day he had seen 315387 on the siding. For a man with little to do, Ed had a rather disorganized office. At least the file drawers had labels.

It took longer than he thought, but he finally found the manifest for the steam consist for the right morning, a line of empty grain cars, two flats with graders and two boxcars, 114296 and 114683 from the furniture factory. At the bottom of the list, someone had pencilled in the number '3'. It did not seem to be part of the manifest list, but it was clearly there. Blatchford laid the file on Ed's desk and tried to think about it.

"What the hell are you doing?" Ed's voice menaced. Bill hurriedly closed the file folder. He had lost track of time and Ed caught him redhanded. He came clean.

"Remember that car 315387 I was asking about? I wanted to see if it was on a manifest." Blatchford stood quickly and circled the far side of the stationmaster's desk. Ed was clinching and relaxing his fists. Bill knew Ed had been born and raised in the railway, had worked it all his life. He probably could fight like a railway man, too. A railway man against an out of practice war vet; Bill thought it might not go well.

"Well, it ain't," Ed plopped into his chair, indignant and defensive. It had tempted him to pound Blatchford out, but the man's knowledge was dangerous and had to be defused. "I've never seen that car or put it on a list. Never let me catch you going through my stuff again, or you'll regret it."

Ed glowered up at Blatchford, trying to look official, trying to hide his fear.

"Well, a train dropped it at 47. Since it wasn't me, it has to be O'Connell. There's something curious about that car. O'Connell's the guy to get involved in something shady."

"I'll look into it." Ed decided he might get Blatchford to leave it alone if he pretended to help him. "I'll let you know what I find."

Bill didn't believe the stationmaster would admit to finding anything, but being caught embarrassed him. Ed would more likely tell O'Connell and whoever else was involved. Now everyone would know he was looking into the mystery of the boxcar.

Bill headed over to the bunkhouse for a shower and a shave. He would soon take Kat for a ride.

Blatchford pulled the '48 Olds into the parking area in front of the water driven grist mill. The car was over ten years old but immaculate, a Dynamic 68 with a Hydramatic transmission. It was almost as good to drive as his Plymouth, but it was a GM. The car stirred up a blast of dust from the powdery surface. Because the Olds was an automatic, Bill drove with one hand, his right arm around Kat's shoulders as she snuggled against him.

The mill, time worn with a pre-war paint job, still functioned when there was water. A Dodge farm truck with peeling wooden racks and a faded red cab sat at the loading dock. Someone had scrawled *Smith Farms* on the door, free-hand, using white house-paint. An old farmer was manhandling sacks of barley into the warehouse.

The railway spur lay on the far side of the road, between the roadway and the furniture loading dock. It was a hump track on a slight hump grade so that gravity could position boxcars along the furniture dock for loading. Three box cars were being loaded. A fourth was sitting a few yards up the track. It was 315387.

"Wait here."

Bill walked over the road and headed to the isolated car. The number 3 appeared to have been hand painted over a patch of railway red that was newer than the boxcar's original paint job. The digit was not as precise as a stencil would have made it. It was closed up, but the door had signs of recent use. He slid it open and looked inside. It was empty.

With his head inside the boxcar, Bill did not hear the crunching of shoes on the railway ballast.

"Who the hell are you?" Someone gave Blatchford a stiff shove on the shoulder. Bill startled and pulled his head from the car. "This is private property, you know."

A short, unfriendly looking man glared up at Bill. He wore a white shirt and tie with no jacket. Several coloured pens stuck up from the shirt pocket. A leaky pen had spread a large blue stain beneath. He held a clipboard and the offending fountain pen in his right hand.

"It's a CSR car," Bill stood his ground, "on CSR track."

"We own the track, buddy. Who are you?"

"I'm Bill Blatchford, the engineer on the diesel from Guelph." Bill extended his hand. The little man ignored it.

"I'm interested in this car." He tapped on the door. "Do you own the car, too? It has been turning up parked at a cattle siding along the Guelph line and now I see it here. The CSR will be wondering. What's the connection?" Blatchford's tone implied a threat.

"You're just an engine driver. I don't need to tell you anything. Get off our property!"

The man wasn't physically threatening. Bill outsized him by a large margin, but he implied the police. Bill was not ready to involve the cops and certainly did not want to do time for assaulting the little twerp. He wanted to go through CSR management and get noticed. Bill quietly walked away as the factory man struggled to close the boxcar door. Bill had come to the mill for another purpose. This was just an unexpected bonus. Blatchford was connecting things. The little man stalked back to the factory, watching Bill and Kat closely.

"You railway guys love boxcars more than girls," Kathleen teased as Bill arrived back at the Olds. "Let's go down by the river," Kat sounded eager. "It's quiet and beautiful there."

"Is it private?" Bill asked.

She carried a car blanket and a little basket of sandwiches and pop. Bill would have preferred beer, but Kat was under drinking age and did not like beer, not since the time her class got drunk after grade thirteen graduation.

They crossed the millrace bridge single file with Kat's hand reaching behind to hold Bill's. Cedars screened the river. A noisy trickle of water leaked through the weir, creating streamers of white foam that floated slowly downstream towards Maitland Station.

Walter Winslow stood on the furniture loading dock watching the lovers wandering through the trees to the river. He was trying to decide what to do. Winslow believed Blatchford had figured out their scheme. He was dangerous and could put them all in jail.

Can I buy him off? He wondered. *We aren't making enough on this, as it is to split it another way. Will he turn us in?*

Winslow decided. He went to his desk in the shipping office and slipped a short-nosed .38 revolver into his pocket.

"I'll be back in a minute," he said to the helper. "Finish these cars and lock them up."

They would not need 315387 for another couple of weeks. They had to slip a few pieces at a time into the production runs to build a shipment slowly, without arousing suspicion. Winslow always struggled to issue fake work orders to the shop with inflated quantities and then replace them with genuine ones in the files to match shipment packing lists and invoices. No one verified the inflated scrap and garbage records.

He walked around the end of a loaded boxcar and headed quickly over the road. The truck that had been unloading grain was gone. He took the catwalk over the mill intakes, keeping the freight cars between him and the furniture loading. Winslow was sure he was not being watched. He checked the gun once more and returned it to his pocket.

He bought the gun shortly after the boxcar operation started. Tough-looking men from Toronto had visited. He had not talked to them, but Walter had heard them threatening the owner. The first shipment had been short, and they were making sure they would fix it in the next load. The men had walked out, arrogant and sure. They were big and mean looking, *Devil's angels*, Winslow had thought then. They had scared him.

Walter crept quietly through the trees, searching for the pair of lovers. His Hush-Puppies were perfect for silent walking on the carpet of dead cedar leaves. He heard the lovers before he saw them. They lay at the water's edge. He forgot himself and rushed, almost tripping on a root. He gasped loudly. The trees and the girl's loud giggling masked his cry. More in control, he peeked through a cedar copse. Blatchford and Kathleen were half naked, entwined on the blanket. Winslow paused, *might as well enjoy the show.*

He watched for a long time as the couple frolicked. He fingered the revolver in his pocket, trying to plan his attack. The erotic scene made it hard to concentrate.

This is better than those magazines from Detroit.

He took out the gun, got through the same route as his skin magazines, and eased forward. His mouth felt dry. His gun-hand trembled. Walter had only fired the gun once, just after he bought it. He had missed the soup can he had set on the fence post as a target. The bullet had gone, God knew where. It had scared him, and he never tried twice. No one had trimmed the cedars here and the lower dead limbs were hard to navigate. He tried not to snap off any as he inched forward.

Winslow was too nervous to get closer. At about ten yards, not realizing that at this range an inexperienced and nervous shooter hitting a target was unlikely, he raised the gun and tried to aim it at Blatchford's back. His target was leaning on one elbow, looking at Kat on the blanket. Winslow fought to steady his shaking hand and squeezed the trigger.

"Click."

Somewhere, probably in a movie, Winslow had heard that they left the first position in a revolver cylinder empty. He had done that without thinking. It probably saved him from being hung, or perhaps being shot with his own gun and thrown into the river.

The sudden fear brought Winslow to his senses. Through his fear and lust filled haze, Winslow realized he would have to kill Kat and the nosy railway man. He couldn't do that. He had known her since she was a baby, her mother Millie, for much longer. The commandment said: *Thou shalt not kill*, at least not to kill young ladies, even if they were wanton sinners. Stoning was supposed to be the punishment for adultery, but Christians were too civilized for that. He would deal with Blatchford when they were alone.

Leaving a distance between him and Blatchford had saved the little man. Bill and Kat had not heard the misfire.

When the pair finished and got dressed, Winslow scrambled away and hurried back to the factory, still afraid. Now that the show was over, the weakness of his flesh disgusted him. From the shadows inside the shipping door, he watched the lovers return, arm in arm. After providing Winslow with more entertainment, fondling and kissing, leaning against the Oldsmobile, the pair drove off.

"What was it about that railcar, and why was the creep Winslow interested?" Kat snuggled contentedly against Bill's arm.

"It has an unusual number, sweetie. It's railway-business. The jerk didn't like me being on factory property."

"He's a self-righteous ass," Kat flared. "He's always bugging Mom and me about going to his church. Mom needed help once, and they refused. They said she was a sinner, and a fallen woman, 'a publican', they said, and no Christian would touch us. It was after that Winslow hounded us. Mom said the louse tried to get her into bed once."

"He seems like a rotten one."

Bill had a good idea what the carried in the boxcar to the siding.

How can I use it to get a promotion? When can I get Kat alone again? I can't wait for a beer. I wonder what Millie's like in bed.

Bill was returning from the hotel to sleep in the bunkhouse. He wanted to spend it in Kat's bed, but that would be too risky with Millie just down the hall. The late August evening was wonderful. Bill was basking in the afternoon's double success and the three glasses of beer he had drunk while flirting with Kathleen. He ignored the car parked beside Ed's Buick. As Blatchford approached, Winslow popped out of the second car.

"Stop right there," his voice was menacing.

Bill glanced around for anyone on the street. All was quiet. He balled his fists and waited.

"Hey, nosy," Winslow was aggressive. His hand gripped the revolver in his pocket. "We need to talk."

"Piss off! You're on my turf now." Blatchford was not as brave as he sounded, but growing up in the depression and army training had taught him attack was always better. Winslow was much smaller. It would be a quick fight. Still, Blatchford remembered his father's admonition to never fight a small man who will fight.

"Why should I listen to a little jerk like you?"

"You'll listen," the gun appeared. Bill froze. He did not know this was the second time Winslow had aimed the pistol at him. He calculated his distance to Winslow and became quiet, needing to close the gap. Blatchford looked around. The lighting was so poor in the station lot someone on the street would have trouble seeing anything. He took a baby step towards the smaller man.

"I didn't like you poking around up at the factory." Winslow stepped towards Bill. He knew nothing about fighting and did not realize he was already within his pistol's killing range. "I'm not saying there was anything to see, but I don't like busy-bodies. You hear?" Bill nodded. Winslow was confirming everything.

"Let's just say you think you saw something and know something," Winslow moved again. Bill thought another yard would do it. "Well, I saw something too, you and that Kat going at it. Millie will be furious with you, a godless sinner, defiling her daughter." He smiled and almost forgot himself thinking of the sex he had witnessed. He carelessly moved closer.

"What do you want?" Bill thought if Winslow intended to kill him, he wouldn't be doing all this talking. Blatchford became more confident.

"Let's just say I can exchange my silence for yours. I won't tell Millie if you forget about the boxcar."

"Kathleen and Millie mean nothing to me. Girls like Kat are a dime a dozen. I couldn't care less."

Bill was getting braver. He eased towards Winslow, trying not to appear aggressive. In the army, his hand to hand instructor had always said, 'surprise and speed, surprise and speed'. Bill suddenly moved. His left hand gripped Winslow's forearm above the gun and his right fist hit the fingers gripping the gun. In his pain, Winslow dropped the weapon into the dust and cried out. Bill turned him around, pulled him back hard against his chest, and wrapped an arm around the little man's neck.

"Game over, Shorty," Bill's voice was derisive, "never try to play in the big leagues again."

He shoved Winslow and tripped him with his left foot. Walter fell into the dust. Bill scooped up the pistol.

"Mine now," he smirked.

Rage filled Walter and hate, humiliation, and helplessness.

Blatchford raised the gun, his thumb searching for the hammer. He heard noisy, half-drunk men approaching the yard. Al's rear-end crew was coming from the beer parlour, heading to their caboose. "You can take your offer and stuff it. When I break this, it will get me a promotion. You'll be in jail."

Bill lowered the gun.

Winslow staggered to his feet. Dust covered him. He was almost in tears.

"You'll find out," he growled. "Millie will want to kill you. I will too. Next time there won't be any talking. Watch your back."

Winslow jumped into his car and roared off in a dusty exit. Bill put the gun into his own pocket.

"Who was that?" O'Connell's conductor, Milt, weaved a bit as he watched Winslow's car disappear.

"It was a guy from the furniture factory. He wanted to sell me a Chesterfield. I told him there wasn't room in the diesel cab."

Blatchford laughed, releasing his tension. The tipsy, uncomprehending men laughed with him. The rails gleamed in the faint streetlight as they stumbled their way across the tracks to the caboose.

Chapter Four

"Why don't you ditch him and come with me?" George Jones reached beneath the sheets for Irene Blatchford. It had been a day of fun. They had driven Blatchford's Plymouth to Fergus for a pleasant lunch and over to Elora for a walk along the gorge. The paths through the trees, abandoned on a weekday, allowed for some intense embraces. The pair had just come up for air after an evening of loving.

"He has full seniority and all the pay and perks. I told you before, I take the best offer." Blatchford's wife rolled over on the bed and looked at Jones. "You're nice, fun and I love you, but I won't leave Bill. If you get full time and Bill is out of the picture, then I'm yours."

"It would be nice to have him out of the way. You know he's sleeping with a young girl at Maitland."

"If I cared, I'd kill him. He's just a meal ticket. He already has a woman at every mile post. I knew that when we got married. He got mad at me once and rubbed it in. That's when I developed a thick skin, and the day I stopped loving him, but I would do nothing stupid like walk out."

"One day, I'll sort him out. He shouldn't be disrespecting you. You deserve better. He'll get his." George Jones hugged Blatchford's wife tightly. She snuggled into his arms.

"Whatever you say, lover," she kissed him, "I'll go along with it."

***

Walter Winslow sauntered into the reception area of Millie's Hotel. Walter had spent a sleepless night planning the encounter, anticipating getting back at Blatchford and confronting Millie at the same time. He was smug. He could not buy the bastard Blatchford, so Millie would get an earful. Winslow thought he might even embarrass the women into joining the church. The Pastor always preached that saving sinners was the best ticket to heaven.

She might even be grateful enough to...

"Walter," Millie frowned. She had hoped he would stop bothering her. He was slime.

"Hello, Millie," he smiled. "Can we talk privately?"

Millie waved her hand in a dismissive gesture, showing Winslow there was no one around.

"What's up, Walter?"

"Kathleen has been sinning with that diesel engineer Blatchford, I think is his name. I saw them yesterday down by the mill," he emphasized the crime. "They were committing adultery."

Winslow frowned, trying to look darkly judgemental. Millie laughed. He looked more like a kid who had been told the black-ball he wanted cost more than the nickel in his pocket.

"So, she's twenty now, a woman. It's her life." Millie was upset, but she would not give this sanctimonious twit any satisfaction. He had quoted too many scriptures to her in the past, all of them adding up to Winslow calling her names.

"You'd better talk to her, and stop it. She's going to hell and you with her. Come to church and seek forgiveness. The Lord said, 'sin no more'".

"I guess sex is a sin, but something like watching naked people having sex or stealing is okay." She stared right into Winslow's eyes.

Winslow looked horrified. His guilty pleasure was being thrown in his face.

"Better be careful, Walter," Millie knew some scripture too. "You might turn into a pillar of salt."

Damn it, thought Winslow, *Al must have told her about what's going on. Damn him!*

He was getting nowhere. Millie didn't care.

"Blatchford knows about the furniture." Walter tried to look conspiratorial and rested his arms on the registration desk. His shortness compelled him to stretch up on the balls of his feet. This was his last hope.

"He says he's going to turn us in."

"What furniture, Walter?" Millie knew, but she didn't want anyone to know that she knew. If it all blew up, and Al went to jail, she wouldn't be involved. Al had not listened to her when the thieving had started. She would not go to jail with him. "Is there something illegal going on I should know about? Is Al in on it? Maybe the cops should investigate."

Winslow turned to go, defeated.

"Walter, get your wife to wash that ink stain out of your shirt," Millie called after him.

Walter rushed out of the doorway, worried Millie might turn them in. They had to quit before Blatchford got any actual evidence. So far all the bastard had was an empty boxcar. He had to tell the boss. Maybe his tough customers could deal with Blatchford. Someone had to.

Winslow almost knocked over Chuck Bisco, who had been standing in the shadows between the outer weather door and the polished oak and glass decorative ones. Chuck had heard it all. Tears streamed down his face. Kat had used his car to have sex with Blatchford. He had always dreamt he and Kat would sit in the car, watching the sunset over Lake Huron and kiss, and she would fall in love with him. It now seemed hopeless. He quietly followed Winslow to the street, cursing Blatchford once again. His hopes and dreams for Kathleen were gone.

Chuck wandered down to the creek and sat on a bench in the shade of a huge maple. He was angry at Kat. He hated the doctor who had destroyed his life. Most of all, Chuck hated Blatchford. He would have to scrub the car from top to bottom. He had savoured the lingering sweetness of her perfume in his car from the previous day and had planned to let it stay as long as possible.

He cried.

Millie called Kathleen into the lobby.

"What the hell were you thinking? Oh, you weren't thinking, just wanting it. Have you ever done it before?"

"No." Kat was subdued.

"With anyone other than Bill, I mean."

"No."

"You and Chuck are together so much, I thought, maybe…"

"Mom, no!" Kathleen was a little too loud.

"It seems to me Chuck would be easy pickings. If I was a cop, I'd say you had opportunity and motive."

"No, Mom. I like Chuck, but he has no prospects."

"When did you become so worldly?" Millie knew she had learned the cynicism from her.

Kathleen looked at her mother. She blushed slightly. She thought Chuck was attractive enough, and he was funny and smart. There was even the time they were at the movies together and almost put Chuck's arm around her shoulders, but she liked him too much to lead him on. She needed prospects.

"You taught me love isn't enough."

"You could get pregnant," Millie ended the tirade. "Boys and men are unreliable. It's dangerous, sleeping around, and there are worse things than having a baby. We don't know Bill at all."

"He's a nice guy, Mom. I love him. He promised to marry me, and we would live in Windsor or Toronto in a big house with a garden and a lawn and a shiny new car in the driveway, when he got on the main line."

Millie frowned. It sounded like the overblown promises of another railway man she knew, liars, every one of them.

"They all promise they'll marry you."

The RS3 roared through, fronting train 100, whistling the crossing just up the street from the hotel. Millie frowned again.

"If you love him and want him, I want to know about him."

Kat went back to the dining room, relieved that it was out in the open, but still not sure her mother was happy about her love. She loved her mother more than Bill, but hoped she would not have to choose.

At the worst, she thought, *Mom and I would work it out. We always do.*

Millie dialled Ed at the station.

"Ed, Kathleen is sweet on that Blatchford guy. What do you know about him?"

"Nothing," was Ed's truthful answer, "aside from not liking him. He has never told me anything personal. I know he doesn't like Al, and Al hates him. Al hates all the diesel guys, though," Ed laughed. Millie was giving her frown a major workout. "He mistreats Chuck Bisco really badly, if that tells you anything."

"I heard about that. It upsets me. Who could I ask in Guelph?" Millie was on a mission.

"Personnel won't tell you anything, but someone in the train-master's office might. I hear lots of gossip whenever I'm down there, nothing about Blatchford though, but they like to talk. Here's the number."

"One more thing," Ed added, "I know he's been flirting with Kathleen. If you want my advice, I wouldn't let him anywhere near her."

Millie hung up. Her frown threatened to become permanent. She hated to pay for the long distance charges during business hours, but Kathleen was worth it. Although her relationship with Albert O'Connell seemed to say otherwise, Millie was a decent judge of character. Something about Blatchford bothered her. Ed had only reinforced it. Blatchford was too smooth.

Chuck was a good kid, too. Hearing that Blatchford could make fun of someone's handicap was not reassuring. Someone trying as hard as Chuck deserved better treatment. Several times she had gone through her accounting, trying to put Chuck on the payroll. There was not enough money. Free meals and pop were all she could muster.

Still, perhaps Blatchford might be the husband for Kat that Millie had never had. Despite her own misgivings, she hoped the man would pass muster. Her fatalism that things in life never worked out was about to be reinforced.

"Can I speak to someone about Bill Blatchford? He's the engineer on train 100."

"Oh, hello," the voice was suddenly warm. "Is this Mrs Blatchford?"

Millie almost dropped the phone, but remained calm and recovered her composure. She had a great deal of experience fielding calls from wives looking for a straying husband who might share one of Millie's rooms with another woman, or, more likely, drunk in the beer parlour. "Yes, it is," she said in her nicest voice.

"Bill left a message for you. He wants you to take the Plymouth to the garage. The brakes are squeaking."

"I will... thank you."

Millie gently laid the handset on the cradle. She stared at the device for several minutes, anger slowly building and her face developing a deeper red. The telephone was not as black as her heart at that moment. She had to tell Kathleen before Blatchford showed up for lunch.

Bastard!

***

Bobby was excited. As soon as they cleared the cars off 111 in the Guelph yard, he rushed to the personnel office. It was only mid-morning. The engineer's course for the diesels was to start in October and he wanted to get his application in.

Walter knew what Bobby was doing. The pair decided not to let on to Al. He was already upset with Bobby for riding with Blatchford. Being an expert on fishy storytelling, Al did not really believe the girlfriend existed.

"She's a cute blond with an enormous chest and an ass that makes waves in the air when she walks," Walter had once told Al, trying to do Bobby a favour by inventing a worthwhile conquest. It had helped a little.

"Look at him," Al had replied, "he'd be lucky to get a spinster schoolteacher, and we have a big surplus of them. There's something going on. I know it."

"Tell them you like working the Goderich sub," Walter advised Bobby as he headed to Personnel. "They're short of qualified guys. Jones is ready to move up and take over the RS3 when Blatchford gets moved. You would likely be a shoo-in for spare board fireman for Jones, and it's a short board, too. It looks good."

"Damn, more years as a spare," Bobby hesitated. "Maybe I shouldn't bother."

"Look, Bobby, in a few years, they will cry for trained diesel engineers. Al and I will retire next year. I bet when we do, the Pacific will be retired and there will be another RS3 or something more modern to replace it. That's why the CSR never replaced the Pacific with an oil fired loco. They would have spent too much money on new fuel tenders and things. Steam is done, my friend."

Bobby was desperate for promotion and job security. It had been a struggle on the pay as a spare brakeman with irregular hours. He rented a seedy room above a hardware store, away from his drunken father, who was always fighting with his mother, and the four younger kids underfoot in their ramshackle house near the stockyard. He could barely afford to live on his own, but he had to. Joe Ellis was a monster. Bobby wanted to take his older sister out of there too, before the old man molested Roberta. He would need a better job and more pay to rent a proper place.

Nothing is ever going to force me back to live with the old man and that hell.

Bobby was confident and easily completed the form. Only one question upset him. *Did the police ever accuse or convict you because of criminal activity?*

Bobby Ellis' hand shook as he wrote, 'no'.

Once he finished in the office, Bobby rushed to the station. His sister was meeting him for lunch before the run back to Maitland.

"Hi, Bobby," Roberta smiled. She was pretty but dressed in cheap Woolworth's clothes and aging shoes. She had a slight bruise on her cheek.

"Did the old man do that?" Bobby kissed her and touched her cheek.

"He's getting worse, Bobby. I'm afraid and more afraid for Mom. He hit us both a few days ago."

"I'll kill him!" Bobby flared.

"Oh no, don't do that, Bobby! You'll just hang and it won't help."

"I'm getting you out of there soon, little sister. Maybe we can get Mom and the kids to come too."

"We can't afford it. He would just hunt us down, anyway. Mom has nowhere to go. There are no safe places and welfare won't help. Some prude downtown quoted some scripture to Mom saying she should submit to her husband."

"I have little time. I'll buy lunch and work it out."

As they headed into the station lunchroom, Bobby dropped a quarter into a little girl's basket as she begged on the platform. It made a satisfying clink against some empty bottles.

***

"Bill, come here." Millie sounded pleasant enough as she beckoned the unsuspecting Blatchford. She had watched until she saw the engineer walking across from the railway yard and had called her bar manager to stand by. The big man was out of sight on the far side of the half wall and flowers.

"I want to ask you something." Bill stood near the counter, smiling. Millie took a step around the counter, holding a heavy brass curtain rod. "Are you married?"

Blatchford's smile disappeared, along with most of the blood in his face. Instinctively, he stepped back. The look of anger building in Millie's face told him lying would do no good.

"Yes," he mumbled.

With no warning, the curtain rod caught him on the side of the head. His arm was too slow to deflect the blow.

"You're a bastard. You're lucky I don't have a gun. Get out and never come back, and keep looking over your shoulder. I might find a gun."

Anger surged, fed by the pain. Bill stepped towards Millie, balling his fist and cocking his arm to strike. A powerful hand grabbed his forearm and twisted his right arm behind his back. A red face, smelling of beer, pickled eggs, and onions pressed against Bill's.

"Not today, buddy. You ain't hitting no woman today, especially one as nice as Millie."

Blatchford's fear masked the lingering pain from Millie's blow. The bar manager was ex-military and had fought in the Korean War. He was over six feet tall, two hundred and forty pounds of muscle. There was a partly true story he had single-handedly killed ten Chinese soldiers in a hand to hand fight.

"Don't you ever come near me or Kat again, or I'll kill you." Millie held the door as the barman sent Blatchford sprawling onto the street. A truck loaded with cream cans swerved, just missing the flattened engineer. The sound of its horn and rattling cans carried over the railway crossing. The driver had seen no one thrown out of Millie's so early in the day.

"You heard the lady," the red-faced barman shut the door.

He turned to Millie. "If you need to deal with that effing scum again, you let me know. He'll be one of my good intentions on the road to hell."

***

"Bobby," Ed called to the brakeman, who had just dismounted from the Pacific fronting Train 110. "Your new tool box came by express this morning. Leave the old one here. I'll get the night man over in the steam shed to pick it up. He's got lots of room for spares."

The Pacific was waiting on the lead opposite the station. Bobby lugged his old tools into the office and dropped the battered wooden box beside Ed's desk. The shiny steel box of hammers and big wrenches would be welcome.

"Would you send Al in before you guys knock off?" Ed asked Bobby as he struggled off with his toolbox. "Tell him it's urgent."

"O'Connell, Bill Blatchford is asking about the boxcar. He's onto something." Ed was standing behind his desk. "I might have put him off, but I'm not sure. I haven't seen him since Tuesday at noon. He was going through the manifests. He said outright you must be the one moving the car." Ed frowned.

"Technically, I'm off the hook, never accepted a cent, just those bottles last Christmas; however, if there's an investigation, it would be obvious I was not paying attention and deliberately ignoring misuse of CSR property at worst. If this ever gets out, management will pin it on everyone they can, covering their own asses."

"Don't worry about Blatchford, Ed. I'll take care of him." Al stalked out. He sent word to everyone that there would be a 'caboose meeting' after dinner. Al headed up to Millie's.

"I see Blatchford didn't hang around today. He was waiting and took my load to Goderich right away, wasn't very talkative either." Al slumped into a chair.

"Damn right the ass never hung about," Millie was red-faced. "He came in here cocky as hell. I was waiting and had Kat upstairs. Blatchford seduced her the other day... bastard! Winslow up at the factory told me. Another bastard. He watched them going at it. I know you have a deal going with him, but if it were up to me, I'd drown him in the river like a rat."

"Kat, having sex wouldn't be that bad, except I checked up. Kathleen loved him, she said, and I wanted to know more about him. I phoned the Guelph despatch office and said I was calling about him. The chick on the other end asked if I was Mrs. Blatchford. I nearly dropped the phone. I was smart enough to say 'yes'. She had a nice domestic message for Mrs. Blatchford." Millie spat out the name and stopped for air. Al's face was red.

"Blatchford confessed. I told him he was a bastard and lucky I didn't have a gun. I told him to get out and never come back, and to keep looking over his shoulder because might find a gun. He was going to hit me, for nothing, well actually, for something; I whacked him on the head with a curtain rod. I had George here just in case. He grabbed him and threw him into the street." She smiled, but tears flowed.

"It devastated Kat. She's up there crying her eyes out."

Al was unusually calm. "I'll fix him," he said. It surprised and scared Millie. Al already hated Blatchford for something to do with the railway, something to do with Guelph. She expected O'Connell to be ranting, swearing, and throwing furniture like he usually did. She had never seen him angry enough to be quiet.

"No one does that to my daughter. Get me a beer."

"Al," Millie had calmed down, "Winslow also told me Blatchford was asking about what's going on with the boxcar. They had a bit of a fight over it. I pretended I knew nothing about it. Al, get out of that mess. You and the guys are going to end up in jail. If you ever say I knew about it, I'll deny it, and you'll end up in the river with Winslow."

Millie looked like she was ready to do it.

"Blatchford has been nosing around at the yard, too. We'll deal with it."

"Well, you had better before the CSR sicks the cops on us. I don't like railway cops."

"That's the first time you called Kathleen your daughter. Folks guessed from her red hair, but I said it was a throwback to my Irish grandmother. You should have owned up all along. She needed a father when she was a little girl. Once she knows you're her father, she might kill you and Blatchford at the same time."

Al quietly sipped three Labatt 50s as he contemplated the mess he had made of his life and Millie's and Kathleen's. He left with his crew, sober as a church mouse, right after dinner.

"Blatchford knows we are up to something." Al was in charge. He had been the one to drag the others into the conspiracy.

The five men spread about the living space of the caboose. Jim and Milt sat on their bunks, Walter and Al in the two chairs and Bobby was hanging his legs from the heavy fixed table. The interior was nicely polished tongue-and-groove pine boards with green and tan checkerboard tile on the floor. There was a squat woodstove for winter heat, but no cooking facilities. The Goderich sub only had short runs. They had not cleaned the interior in months.

"Bobby," Al glared at the brakeman, "did you say anything while riding with that bastard?"

"Not a word. The subject never came up. Jones told me once that Bill had seen the boxcar at the siding, but he said nothing else."

"Well, he got interested. Winslow at the factory had a set-to with him. Blatchford said he was going to use it to get promoted."

"We all have everything to lose," said Walt. "We have to stop right now. He'll have the railway cops breathing down our necks. We have to stop him, somehow."

"He doesn't have any evidence," Al said, "but he could still cause us trouble. Even a black mark on our records could hurt us, especially you younger guys who aren't about to retire."

"They might just retire Al and I early," Walter said. "You younger guys will get fired and at worst be in jail along with Winslow. He's the guy who's really on the hook, but you all could end up doing serious time in Kingston."

"So would the owner," said Al. "He's in on it."

"The owner," Bobby asked, "why would he steal from himself?"

"You didn't think Winslow could pull this off without the owner, did you? Walter's too stupid and has no connections. The owner controls all the paperwork to make it happen and wins in two ways. He gets to write off the extra material purchases against taxes, and he pockets the cash, no taxes paid. It's slick. They just duplicate an order once in a while. He's selling to some seriously dangerous guys. I hope they never find out about any of us."

"Why don't the auditors catch it?"

"I think he buries the material as wastage. He has no share-holders to convince. Both guys would fall big time to the federal tax man. The owner is the only one who knows who the buyer is. From what Winslow says, I would bet he wouldn't make it to trial." Al stood. "The upshot of it all is we would all be out of jobs."

"I can't afford that," Bobby said. Everyone nodded in agreement.

After an hour of discussion, they agreed Al would go see Winslow before another shipment to tell him they were through. Everyone knew to keep their mouths shut.

"I'll get to Winslow next week. I'll sort out Blatchford too. The bastard won't like it."

The men settled down for a restless night.

Al headed back to Millie's. He knew he had to face Kathleen.

What can I say? Will she hate me because I never was a father to her, or will she hate me because Al O'Connell is her father? Damn Winslow! Damn Blatchford!

Chapter Five

That week, the Canadian Southern Railway, in all of its wisdom, reversed the flow of the combination 101 and 100. 101 would now go east to Guelph in the morning, followed by 111 which had to be held back at Maitland until 8:33 AM.

Al's crew would no longer have the leisurely turn around in Guelph but would pick up train 110 and leave Guelph after lunch to arrive in the Goderich yard by 3:37 in the afternoon. Bobby was happy they would run the bridge again. 1232 would bring all the waiting freight cars back to Maitland and squared away before 100 ran through. The westbound evening combination would arrive in Goderich about 8:30PM, after dark.

Blatchford had to overnight in Goderich. He was no longer welcome in Millie's Hotel, and Bill was afraid O'Connell would actually beat him, or worse. Maitland Station was a flag stop for his trains. If someone had to go into the station, Bill would send his fireman.

Jones lost his all day visits with Blatchford's wife and had to be well clear of his home by sunup on the two nights he booked off on the spare board. Bill would go home between his runs. Blatchford was getting underfoot.

Blatchford seemed unmoved by the schedule change. It was a minor inconvenience. He was more concerned with working from his journal, trying to frame his suspicions in just the right way to affect his career. He would stop and check the car the next time he saw it on the siding.

Bill would soon run a modern locomotive on the Windsor-Toronto line where the changeover from steam was almost complete.

Blatchford struggled with the fact he had no proof of anything. A bit of actual evidence would be helpful. He kept hoping to see the boxcar at Mile 47, but in the next week it did not appear. If everything was normal, it would turn up at the end of the month, in one week. He would arrange for a trap.

****

Train 100 eased out of Guelph station at precisely 6:01 PM. They had to be in Goderich by 8:30. Not that long of a run, but the evening schedule created a passenger demand from Guelph to Elmira, and several smaller towns, like Monkton and Blyth. People found it convenient to take 101 in the morning, do business or go shopping and even connect to Toronto. The 6:01 made it easy for travellers to return the same day. The resulting stops added to the time needed for the train to make Goderich.

It was a fine August evening. George Jones was enjoying the ride. The signals were always 'high-clear', but he had to keep his eyes open for a flag pickup, although they were rare.

"Damn this sun!" said Blatchford. "I'm almost too late whistling at the crossings. These farmers had better be looking." He pulled his American military sunglasses from their pouch. Women thought they were attractive. They worked well.

Damned yard man should have cleaned this window. Blatchford put the glasses on and pulled his ball-cap down to shade his eyes.

"Like you're riding off into the sunset," George laughed, squinting beneath the peak of his railway hat, watching the left rail. He sneaked a glance at Blatchford. Bill riding into the sunset would suit George.

***

The fear of what might happen because of Bill Blatchford snooping around about the boxcar had everyone in Al's crew on edge. The Pacific seemed to drag along the tracks. Time passed as if each tick of the clock would mean doom. They wrapped up dinner at the hotel before seven. Everyone left for the yard, except Al. As usual, he would spend the night with Millie.

"Millie, I have to go see Winslow at the factory. Can I borrow your car?"

"If you promise to tell him, you won't haul the stolen furniture anymore." The furniture business was dragging on her. No matter how he handled it, Millie was about ready to throw Al out of her life. When she thought about it, the only good thing he had ever given her was Kathleen. He had been an absent father, even though he had seen his daughter almost every day of her life. Kat had never experienced the fun and wisdom that a father was supposed to share with his children. Millie remembered her own father with love. She was creating a fantasy in her mind of Al being jailed for some crime, possibly because of Blatchford, and sparing her the effort of putting her shoe into his ass.

"I plan to tell Winslow we're through." Al stood and held out his hand. Millie gave him the keys. "I'll be back about nine, if Winslow's on time."

Al sprayed gravel out of the hotel parking lot and turned west around the corner at the Supertest. It was going away from the factory, but he had to sort things out before seeing Winslow. He needed strength to fix the problem.

Blatchford ran the RS3 under the tunnel at Blyth and through the yard to Highway 4. They were a few minutes behind, and he cheated above yard speed.

"You're a little fast here, Bill." George hung nervously out his window, hoping a stray dog or kid was not in the way.

"The hell with these local hicks," scoffed Blatchford. "Who cares about them?"

God, thought Jones, *I hate this guy. I'll soon have his job, and he'll be out of her life for good.*

Blatchford whistled for the crossing at the highway and threw the throttle up a notch, speeding towards Maitland Station, ten minutes away.

The rear end crew climbed into the caboose. Walter and Bobby headed for the bunkhouse. The early evening shadows filled the yard. A streetlight gleamed from the windshield of Ed's Buick. The light at the engine shed reflected from the polished rails of the main. The sun was well below the trees.

"Walter, what'll I do if I lose this job?" Bobby sounded scared. "No one will ever hire me if I have a record. I have to get Roberta out of Dad's house."

"I don't know, Bobbie. The whole thing's a mess we never should have gotten into. Al's the one who dragged me in. You just landed in it by accident when you came off the spare board. Maybe the cops would go light on you."

Bobby seemed nervous and thoughtful.

"Damn, I left my kit in the engine." Walter stopped at the bunkhouse door. "I'll see you later." He headed towards the engine shed. The night man would not be in until later.

As bunkhouses went, the Maitland one was a luxury with private rooms. Snoring, all too common because of the closeness of Millie's beer parlour, would keep no one awake. When Walter returned, Bobbie's door was closed. All was quiet. He showered and his bed comforted him. Five in the morning could come with a rush. He was toweling off when train 100 screamed through with its air-horn blasting an unnecessarily long wail. *Damned Blatchford,* Walter thought. *He's rubbing it in.*

By the time they reached Maitland Station, the sun was behind the trees. The semaphore was 'high-clear', the station and empty parking lot abandoned to the night with only the safety light at the engine shed visible on the far side of the yard. They roared across the main street with the air horn wailing in a long lament. Blatchford gave it an extra second to annoy anyone at Millie's Hotel. Jones was happy when they passed the yard limit marker, but he could not relax.

The river crossing beyond Maitland Station was beautiful in the fading evening light. The banks hid in black shadow, and the low water reflected the green and purple of sunset. George watched some ducks looking for a last morsel before settling into places where an approaching fox or coyote would splash out a warning.

A gentle flow of mild air snaked through his open window, carrying the pungent smell of river mud. The pounding of the trestle gave way to the clacking of rail joints as they snaked along the contour through farm fields. Light from the headlamp illuminated the rails, but quickly died in the greenery along the roadbed. There was a crossing every mile or so. The lingering lament of the diesel horn filled the valley.

To George, it seemed an evening from a story. He remembered those picture books as a child, mostly of English railways, but romantic and beckoning. He had been born with a railwayman's heart. Sunset had always given him a feeling of foreboding. Perhaps he should write that adventure story he always dreamt of, being lost and surviving in the north woods, fighting bears and wolves. He had always wanted a farm. Maybe one of these flanking the track hidden in the evening shadows might be a better choice.

Bill had the throttle in the eighth notch. They would soon be in Goderich, heading to the bunkhouse, reactivated and cleaned up after the schedule change for train 100.

It isn't Irene's bed, but it's survivable. It won't be long, thought Jones.

There was no traffic on Highway 21. Bill throttled down and fanned the brakes as they entered the even darker tunnel of trees along the high riverbank. The river, far below, reflected the last glint of the western sky through the dark trunks of the oaks and maples. Once they cleared Meneset station, it would be a quick roll over the river and down to the harbour.

"Damn," exclaimed Bill as the Meneset semaphore came into view, "I have to go into the station."

The semaphore often signalled a passenger pickup stop, usually a yard man who lived above the station. Tonight, the train orders signal was also red. It was mandatory that the engineer go into the station and phone down to the Goderich station before going past the signal. This was one signal Blatchford would never ignore.

"Perhaps there's some emergency work going on along the line," Bill scowled.

The RS3 eased to a stop with the hissing of air and squealing of brake shoes against steel wheels. The cars behind banged together as the knuckle slack filled. It was an unexpected stop, and Bill had braked hard. He could imagine the few passengers in the back cursing as packages ended up on the floor. Because of the downgrade, Blatchford set the train air brakes and the ones on the diesel. No passenger was waiting. He hung his sunglasses on the brake handle and opened his door.

Bill's boots crunched on the gravel of the rude platform as he stalked impatiently the ten yards along the boxcar from the engine to the station entrance. They made these small country station platforms of gravel covered with fine stone, held in place by creosoted timbers along the track, with sloping ramps at each end. The wooden floor of the station porch lay under an overhang supported by a bolted timber-frame. Paint was curling and flaking off the poorly maintained building. Cracked and worn planks ended above an equally weathered single wooden step. The timbers supporting the roof still held the brackets for long abandoned oil lamps. The cast iron showed scratches from countless strike anywhere matches as impatient travellers lit their smokes. A yellowing bare light bulb, near to burning out, shone from the enamelled white reflector of a hat fixture, dark green on the outside. A gooseneck pipe held the lamp clear of the wall above the door. Moths made the light flicker as they frantically danced around the glowing bulb.

Bill walked through the doorway. He was impatient at this unusual delay. The interior was gloomy and empty. The corners hid in shadow dark enough to hide the devil. Blatchford did not feel threatened. He confidently made his way through the gloom and pulled out the key to unlock the call box. He fumbled for a minute, trying to locate the key slot in the lock. Bill finally used his cigarette lighter. His shadow danced against the far wall. Beady rat's eyes gleamed out from under the cold woodstove in the corner, the nervous animal biding its time.

On the far side of the train, hidden by the boxcar, someone pulled the lever, extracting the knuckle pin on the coupling between the engine and the train. They secured the handle in the open position with a piece of wood, lashing it with baling wire, and headed along the gangway to the fireman's cab door.

"Look, Jenkins, the banjo told me to call," Bill shouted.

"Well, there's no need. I didn't do it. Come on down." It irritated Jenkins at the Goderich station. The telephone had interrupted him, listening to the Tigers running up a good lead on the Yankees.

Blatchford stalked back along the gravel platform, up the engine gangway, and through the engineer's door.

"That damned signal broke or someone's playing games. There was no order." He pulled the door shut and turned towards George Jones. His eyes widened, and his right hand reached into his pocket, closing about the handle of the little .38. He drew the pistol from the pocket.

"What the hell?"

Those were Blatchford's last words. The heavy wrench connected hard against his temple. Bill crumbled to the engine floor. Two more blows ensured he was truly dead. Blatchford made an involuntary gasp and then lay silent. The snub nosed.38 had fallen from his hand. It ended up and stuffed into another's pocket and they lifted his body onto the engineer's seat, his arms hung loosely to the sides. They jammed the heavy wrench down, depressing the dead-man's foot switch. They set the drive to forward. Blatchford's sunglasses clattered to the floor as the engine brakes released and the throttle moved to the first notch. There were two short blasts on the air horn as the engine rolled ahead. Air hissed as the airline to the boxcar snapped apart. They pushed the throttle up to notch five. The engine protested at the rough treatment, but the diesel blew black smoke and the big electric drive motors responded. A lone figure slipped out the rear door, along the short-hood, and jumped from the speeding train to the roadbed.

"Oh!"

The assailant's feet hit the ballast with the engine moving faster than expected. Darkness obscured the ground. The killer fell forward. Their body slid on the rough ballast beside the track, only slightly softened by decaying leaf litter.

The abandoned train sat in the gloom about thirty yards behind. The RS3disappeared into the night towards the bridge.

The surprised conductor looked out the Dutch door above the front step of the passenger coach. Harold heard the two horn blasts and expected the train to be moving. It sat motionless, with none of the expected hiss of the air brakes or the jolting as the hitch knuckles stretched after the stop. There was nothing visible. The platform, poorly lit by the door light, sat empty. In the gloom, he thought he saw someone limping up the roadway behind Meneset Station.

Impatiently, Harold folded the step cover and flipped the door open. He grabbed his flashlight and headed to the front of the train. In the upper parking lot, car lights blazed. The vehicle quietly moved away into the night. In a few steps, the conductor realized he had no engine. Harold broke into a run towards the station, fumbling for his own key to the phone box. Through the darkness, he heard the RS3, a mile away, rumbling across the bridge.

Locomotive 8439 surged down the grade to the river and ran the curve with a slight lean onto the bridge, gaining speed with every second. The down-slope and the lack of draw weight allowed the engine to speed up quickly. It curved off the end of the bridge, rushed across the North Harbour Road overpass and flew along the base of the bluff.

The headlamp came in sight of the station just as Abe Jenkins, the stationmaster, answered Harold's frantic phone call from Meneset.

Damn, what's going on up there?

In the background, Al Kaline was at bat with a three and zero count, home-run territory and two men on. It was only eight thirty and into the middle innings. The Yankees had come back to tie the game.

"... and here's the pitch," George Kell's voice came from the old Deforest-Crosley radio.

Abe picked up the phone. The crack of a bat came from somewhere behind. The rumble from an approaching train grew louder.

People waiting on the platform for a passenger turned eagerly towards the diesel's headlamp rounding the corner of the bluff. The realization came slowly. All was not right. The train moved too fast. There was no bell, no warning blast from the air horn, or the sound of braking. Onlookers flattened against the wall. One ran behind the station.

"That's the third time this season that Kaline has..." Kell's voice faded in Jenkins' growing puzzlement.

Abe dropped his phone and rushed to the door in time to see the RS3 speed past. He was about to run for the back door when he realized the locomotive was on its own. Train 100 was nowhere in sight. He stepped onto the platform and watched in helpless fascination.

The diesel rattled over the frog of the second lead switch and seconds later smashed hard into the spare passenger coach parked on the runout. Jenkins saw a fan of debris fly away from the impact and the roof of the old coach rise above the hood of the RS3.

The car surged forward with 8439 firmly wedged into its end. Then the coach's first wheel hit the derail, and the car jumped into the air and went to the ground. The weight and momentum of the locomotive drove the combination hard into the buffer, causing the pair to roll with the front of the coach going left and swinging the embedded locomotive to the right. The RS3 crashed onto the engineer's side.

The rear engine trucks had twisted the rails from the sleepers before the heavy drive assembly came loose from the frame and flew off into the night. Bright electric arcs lit the scene for an instant as the heavy power leads parted. The passenger car had broken free at the buffer and twisted even more.

The heavy diesel engine under the long-hood dragged the twisted mess into an increasing angle. It plowed up a furrow, ballast and debris flying in every direction, before coming to a halt. For a few seconds, the sound of falling debris came from the darkness.

The sound of shattering glass, metal, and wood ceased, leaving a pall of dust and smoke over the wreck. Silence descended as the air tank pressure hissed to zero and the diesel stopped as the fuel lines emptied. The evening lake breeze wafted the cloud up the hill towards the town.

"Hello, hello, hello?" Harold, still clutching the handset in the Meneset station, had heard the crash through the phone. A few seconds later as the sound came up the river and caught up to the phone signal.

"Hello, hello, hello?" Then the line went dead. Harold laid the handset on the cradle.

Jenkins frantically dialled the Goderich volunteer fire department. He then ran towards the wreck, clutching a Pyrene fire extinguisher. The smell of diesel was heavy, but he couldn't see any flames. Diesel was not very combustible. If it had been a steamer, there would be hot coals and fire everywhere, live steam to avoid, and men screaming in agony. Likely, the crew would have burned to death or cooked in the steam.

The long-hood had peeled up and folded onto the cab, while cowling from the rear hood littered the ground. One of the braver bystanders caught up to Jenkins, and the pair came to a stop near the remains of the engine cab. There was no safe way to get to the fireman's door hanging open above their heads. They stood dumbfounded, watching diesel fuel gush from the ruptured tank as the sounds of sirens grew behind them.

"Holy Cow!" the first firefighter on the scene exclaimed. Then he smelled the diesel.

"Get those foam extinguishers. Quick." He ran back to his truck.

"That little piss pot wouldn't have done much." The firefighter smiled from beneath his hat. "You would have been just spitting on it if there had been a fire."

Abe Jenkins sat on a step at the station, shaking and bewildered, clutching his unused extinguisher.

"Lousy parking job," the fire chief laughed, covering his own shock.

Abe sat, stunned. Everything had happened too fast. The small crowd of onlookers swelled as people rushed down from the town, following the sirens. Some claimed they had heard the crash. Those expecting loved ones on the train were relieved to hear someone temporarily marooned them at Meneset.

"If the train had remained attached, it would have destroyed the station and killed us." Abe shook even more.

"The only one dead is the guy in the engine." The firefighter shuddered, his attempt at humour forgotten. He wasn't used to seeing bodies.

"There should have been two. Who was in the cab?"

"We need you to tell us."

Jenkins reluctantly went with the man to the engine. They had laid the body on a tarp near the road. The cab had not suffered too much damage, but the left side of the locomotive looked almost normal, and the crash had badly broken and bloodied the victim.

"It's Blatchford, the engineer. Where's Jones? He was the fireman onboard tonight."

A firefighter covered Bill's bloody body. Abe stepped away, trembling.

"We're searching to see if it threw him clear." Several bobbing flashlights acknowledge the search on both sides of the destroyed track. The spotlight of the pumper moved slowly over the ground.

"Someone had better walk back along the track to Meneset. Maybe he jumped when the engine went out of control."

"How can these things go out of control?" asked the firefighter.

"I don't know. Maybe the brakes failed, but it sounded like it was under power when it hit. Something or someone really screwed up. Look for Jones in the river."

***

Millie's car pulled into the front lot of the furniture factory and sprayed gravel as it made a wide swinging turn and pulled up, barely missing Winslow. It was about ten past nine. Al was late. The headlights streamed through the clouds of dust left by a dry August. Al left the engine running,

"Where have you been?" Winslow stood beside his own car and was unhappy. He had an idea why O'Connell had asked to meet. "I was about to leave. This is a good TV night."

"Good thing you didn't. I was driving around, thinking," Al did not offer a hand. "We need to stop this thing now."

"You're spooked by that Blatchford guy. Don't worry about him," Winslow managed a smile. "He can't do anything."

"He isn't a problem," Al agreed. "He couldn't prove nothing. Someone else might take notice though, and they might actually find something."

"Look," said Winslow, "I agree. I talked to the boss. He doesn't like it, but he's worried too. He has committed to at least one more shipment in the next week or two. After that, I think we're done, at least for a bit, until Blatchford disappears."

"The guys that the boss deals with are heavy hitters from Toronto, not nice guys. He fears them. We can't risk getting them mad. They might not let us quit now. Even if they don't rough us up, all they need to do is to threaten to go to the tax man."

"Blatchford might disappear sooner than we think. We all got in too deep," muttered Al. "We'll do one more. It should be safe enough now. I'll tell the guys. After that, you tell your boss he'll have to send it out by truck."

Winslow walked away. Al followed him.

"Oh, one more thing," Winslow turned. Al's fist struck Walter's mouth. The little man went down hard onto the dusty gravel. "That's for watching Kathleen naked. That's how I deal with anyone who defiles my girl. You ain't the first guy I've hit over Kat. Never come near her or Millie again."

Al roared off in Millie's car, spraying gravel over Winslow as the bleeding man tried to stand up. He eventually limped to his car.

Where the hell is my gun?

Chapter Six

When Al O'Connell wandered across the street from Millie's at five in the morning, it surprised him to see the passenger coach and express car parked on the main in front of the station. He thought he had heard a steam locomotive whistle at the crossing in the middle of the night, but had put it down to a dream. He needed a few beers once he returned to the hotel and had gotten drunk. Millie made him sleep in his own room for it. Not even his description of the agreement with Winslow cheered her up, although she had smiled when Al told her he'd laid the little twerp in the gravel. She hadn't said a word as he ate breakfast.

Georgie was hissing on the shed track, waiting. Ed came out of the station and intercepted Al.

"What's this all about?" Al waved at the parked combination.

"Quiet, you'll wake Harold and his crew. They're sleeping in the express car. There was a terrible accident at Goderich last night. Blatchford's dead and Jones is missing."

O'Connell smiled.

"Henry brought these cars up with 6275. You're taking the combination to Guelph, behind your manifest. Goderich station is closed. Tonight, you'll bring it all back and run the passengers and express down to Meneset at least, unless they clear the Goderich station. It tore the track up at the second lead switch. We'll be stopping there until they finish the repairs at Goderich. You're supposed to leave here at 8:31 just like 101 did. They're bussing passengers up from Goderich and along the line."

"What happened?"

"8439 dropped the train at Meneset and sped through Goderich station, hit the passenger car on the dead end and they both wrecked, tore up that track and the far lead switch. Everything else is fine. Someone disconnected the rest of the combination in Meneset, and it sat there until 6275 took it down and brought these cars here. Henry looked pretty tired. He says it's chaos down there, firefighters and cops everywhere."

"When you get the combination made up, come see me. Get the coach off the main. Wait for a work train coming up from Guelph."

Al went to the engine. Walter was tending the fire and Bobby was busy oiling wheel bearings. Milt and Jim waved from the caboose. No one seemed to be upset when Al told them Blatchford was dead.

"Where's Jones?" asked Bobbie, "I liked him."

"Missing," said Al. "Maybe he's the guy who unhooked the engine."

"Maybe Blatchford did that and they'll find Jones dead in the river. Maybe someone murdered them both."

"Walter, shut up!" said Bobby. "Why would someone murder them?"

"I know several reasons," Al muttered.

"Did the locomotive go into the river?" Bobby asked.

"No, it went through the station and took out the spare coach on the stub."

"I always thought a wreck there would be at the bridge," Bobby frowned as he climbed onto the rear ladder of the tender, ready to hook up.

They hurried to make up train 101 plus the manifest freight. It took some imagination to decide how to put it together. In the end, they would hook the passenger and baggage car right behind 1232 and have the caboose with Milt and Jim on the back end as if it were 111.

The coach had to be available on the platform track for ten minutes before leaving, but before that they parked it on the lead, out of the way of the work train that rushed west somewhere between Guelph and Maitland Station.

Al put the assembly onto the lead. They watched as the work train, flying white flags from an RS1 switcher, sped through the station. A flat bed of rail, another of switch parts, fronted the heavy lift crane with its own power unit. A regal caboose that belonged to the road-manager was just in front of a work gang coach and a standard working caboose. The fancy car served as office and bedroom whenever the road-manager had to be away from Guelph.

"I guess it's serious if Fancy Dan is attending." Al didn't like the road-manager. He was too by the book for the engineer. He kept complaining that the heavy Pacific was hitting the switch frogs too hard.

When the work consist passed, Al put the passenger coach to the platform and scurried about, setting his own caboose on the engine shed wye. They couldn't block Main Street for twenty minutes, so they waited for the departure time. It took ten minutes to reconnect everything, so they headed east, fifteen minutes late. Al looked out behind.

"At least we get to do a passenger run again," he smiled at Walter and Bobby. Heavy black smoke curled back, smothering the coach and express car. All the windows were closed.

***

Mike Donovan was an early riser. It was a habit from his days in the RCMP, policing lonely outposts in the far north. He had not changed his schedule simply because he was now a railway cop in a comfortable town apartment. His scrambled eggs were almost ready when the phone rang. Mike gave the device a stare as if it was some rude intruder. One advantage up north: there were no phones and the radio system was intermittent. He lifted the handset.

"Come in to see me when you get to the office," Byng Webster, Mike's boss, sounded tired. "There was a fatal accident at Goderich last night with a lot of damage to company property. I'll need to send you up."

"Who died?"

"Oh, some engineer. I'll fill you in."

Donovan scowled at the phone. He did not like his boss. Mike usually had little to do with Webster. It was the best thing about their relationship. He guessed the man involved Donovan because the CSR was afraid of getting sued and wanted all the facts. Most of the CSR police force comprised cousins and brothers of managers. Mike Donovan was the only trained investigator they had in Guelph.

Donovan was a meticulous dresser. The Mounties trained him that way. He had used the routine of always dressing in perfectly adjusted, clean uniform and polished boots to avoid madness from the isolation and the depressing work in those remote northern outposts.

Many constables became sloppy when away from civilization. Mike felt it made them sloppy in their work, too. The added impetus was the memory of his mother always telling him to look good. She would pinch lint off his Sunday suit and polish scuffs off his shoes with her own handkerchief before going into mass. His tie had to be perfect and his cap clean and set straight. That school-boy cap had given way to a Mountie's Stetson and now to a tweed fedora that always sat straight. As an only child, he had received more fussing than the other kids. Most of them at church or school had six or seven brothers and sisters.

Mike straightened the knot of his tie and walked into his boss' office. He politely removed his hat and stood waiting. His boss had never been a cop. The room did not look like a policeman's space. It reminded Donovan of a banker's office. Webster worried more about money and excessive overtime than policing.

Byng Webster had been an adjutant for a stay at home Canadian General in the last war. He had been born in 1917 but had inherited none of the competent or caring traits of the famous British General they had named him after. He got the job at the CSR through his political connections. After the war, insiders had the fast track to cushy management jobs. Webster was no exception. Family ties and political connections led to the situation where Donovan reported to a younger man. Mike had wondered if his boss was also a Mason, usually a prerequisite for promotion in Canadian companies. He discounted the possibility. If Webster had been a lodge member, he and Donovan, a descendant of Irish Catholics, would have had more to fight about. Webster was often rude and condescending, but never hostile.

"Sit."

Mike sat.

Webster continued to examine a document. Mike broke the ice.

"What's going on with this wreck, Mr. Webster?" The RCMP forced a formal relationship between officers and constables. Donovan could not break the habit, even with his rather dubious boss. Byng Webster did not encourage informality. He sat erect and silent for a good minute, emphasising his importance and rank.

"There was a lot of damage up at Goderich. According to the road-manager, the dead engineer wrote off the RS-3, a total loss. The fireman is missing. The local cops are searching for him. There is every chance they will find him in the river or washed out into the lake. There is a boat out now."

"Blatchford had a wife who could sue us over this. We want all the details wrapped up. Do what you need to do, but don't spend too much money. You can stay in the bunkhouse at Goderich."

"I don't stay in bunkhouses." Mike frowned. Webster was being accidentally insulting. Donovan put his foot down on staying in dirty, road-crew accommodations. "I'll book a hotel."

There was little danger Webster would refuse. He had no one else he could trust to put together a file that he might need in court. He could bully the rest of his rag-tag police force, but not Donovan. The accident was in the jurisdiction of the Goderich cops, but they always called in the Provincials on tough cases. Webster needed work that some sharp lawyer could not tear apart. Still, he frowned.

"Make sure it's a traveller's hotel."

The establishments where salesmen stayed were usually cheap but often poorly kept and dirty.

"For sure." Mike saw no purpose in arguing. He would book into a place he found suitable. "I'll be frugal."

"You'll be dealing with the local hick police chief," Webster looked at a paper. "His name's Bowers. Good luck and make it quick."

Donovan stood to go. He almost saluted. "Do I drive there?"

"We run a train every day. Take it instead. It's cheaper. Keep all your receipts for approval."

Mike Donovan eased the CSR Chevy to a gentle stop behind Guelph station. They painted the car white with the railway logo on the doors and the word 'Police' beneath. There were no pursuit lights. Law forbid the railway police force to patrol public roadways. Mike extracted his overnight bag and briefcase from the back seat, pulled down his jacket sleeves, adjusted his fedora, straightened his tie, and headed to the platform.

A casual observer would think Donovan was a dandy. It was a warm summer afternoon, but the detective wore a brown herringbone jacket that matched the fedora. His white shirt gleamed and the necktie in railway maroon, tied in a precise Edwardian knot, circled his neck beneath a starched collar. Grey flannel pants with a sharp crease covered his ankles, ending at the meticulously polished black shoes. He carried a newly polished leather suitcase. Only the briefcase stood out, battered and somewhat flabby from years of use. The case had the monogram, now fading, of the RCMP. He was clean shaven. Donovan's skin had a red tint to it, as if he was working hard. It was more his Irish ancestry fighting for recognition. Freckles dominated his nose and cheeks. He had once contemplated a beard, but when he had tried it up north it had looked ridiculous, flaming red like some pirate. His Cree friends had made fun.

They said it made him look like he had come north with Sam Steele. He quickly shaved.

Mike walked up the platform along the side of the passenger coach. The car glistened in traditional railway deep green with maroon stripes above and below the windows, but instead of the traditional subdued gold lettering, 'Canadian Southern Railway' above the windows and the name of the coach 'Goderich' below the line of windows were both painted in garish canary yellow.

"Hello, Mr. Donovan," the conductor greeted Mike at the coach step.

The conductor was the uniformed equivalent of Donovan's precise dress. He had polished his shoes to a gleam, pants pressed and his railway vest, tie and waistcoat were immaculate. His peaked pill-box cap had twin gold stripes and the embroidered letters, 'CSR'. His dress was not the careless, food spattered, seldom cleaned cartoon that one often saw on the branch lines. As expected, with older passenger conductors, he was portly and his belly threatened to burst the buttons on his vest. This forced his watch pocket to the front so the watch-stem and gold chain drew one's eye. He smiled beneath wire-rimmed glasses. To the detective, Harold, in his conductor's uniform, looked like he was from some American movie.

"Hello, Harold," Donovan stopped. A trainman grasped his bag. Mike hung onto his briefcase. "Call me Mike. I grub a cheque just like you."

"What's with this ghastly yellow writing?" He waved at the coach.

"It was Goderich's one hundred and twenty-fifth anniversary year. The powers that be," Harold seemed to smirk, "thought it would be a nice way to honour them. They thought they would get more riders, but they're going by Grey coach now, more convenient. It's a bugger to keep clean." To emphasize the point, Harold took out a large white handkerchief and mopped his brow. "That was a few years ago, and they didn't bother to repaint it."

"I guess there's no air-conditioning on this coach." Donovan noted the open windows. Harold looked at Mike's heavy jacket and laughed.

"Sit on the shady side. Once we get going, close the damned window or you'll choke on the smoke. We're back behind a stream engine until they locate a spare line-diesel." "I guess you're going up to Goderich because of the accident, nasty business."

"Yes. When there is so much railway property destroyed and a death there must be an official report. It's likely only a formality, but I'll be there a night or two. It depends on the lay of the land."

"They found the fireman an hour ago in awful shape up near Meneset station. That's a puzzle. At least he's alive. Webster thought he was dead in the river."

The big Pacific engine sat spitting and sighing towards the far end of the platform beside the Guelph freight office. Six boxcars separated 1232 from the express car and a day coach. Behind this combination, a long line of filled grain cars stretched to the caboose. O'Connell and the train-master's clerk watched Donovan walk up the platform.

O'Connell looked impatiently at his watch. In the crisis, they had changed the schedule to combine trains 100 and 110 leaving in the middle of the afternoon. This would last until they found a replacement for locomotive 8439. Al had already lost twenty minutes waiting for this man. His orders were not to leave without him. The new arrival seemed to be in no hurry.

It's as if he owns the damned railway, thought O'Connell.

Finally, the cop shook Harold's hand and boarded. Harold waved all clear to O'Connell, grabbed his portable step and climbed into the coach.

"What a dandy," O'Connell muttered to the clerk and scaled the Pacific's ladder.

The air brakes hissed, accompanied by two blasts from the steam whistle. The drive wheels rotated, stretching the train with clanking and then the squealing of steel on steel. As usual, the heavy load of grain cars caused the drive wheels to spin, throwing sparks and blasting steam sideways. Walter furiously shoveled coal into the firebox. Georgie was hungry for steam on these heavy starts. After several tries, the train rolled. The bell would clang until they cleared the yard.

"I have a long list to interview," Donovan pulled a large notebook from his case, "including you, Harold." He showed the conductor his list, frowned and reached down to rub some dust from his shoe. He tried to remember not to cross his legs. It always wrecked his pant crease.

"Those first five work at Goderich," said Harold, "but I think only the stationmaster was on duty when Blatchford crashed. They called Henry in on the switcher once they realized it had left us at Meneset." Harold yawned. It had been a very uncomfortable night in the baggage car.

"The rest are train crew, Jones, of course, but the others are on this train. I was the conductor last night."

"They cut the train out at Meneset. What happened?" Donovan had learned in his years with the Mounties that sometimes it was good to ask an open question first and let a witness ramble. Things might come out he would never have thought about. Detailed questions could come later.

"It was really a normal run until Meneset, although Blatchford leaned on the air horn a lot going through Maitland Station. He had a fight with some locals and O'Connell's crew. I think he was annoying them. He always said the steam guys were losers. That they were fading out, and he was the future."

"Anyway, we stopped in Meneset. The semaphore called for Blatchford to go in and call for orders. It was unusual, but I thought maybe they had some unexpected track work or some other problem. It was a false alarm, as we know now. The signals must have failed. He didn't reset them, so I guess there was a problem with the mechanism. I watched Blatchford come out of the station and get onto 8439. I sat down. There were only six passengers, and they were nose deep in a newspaper or fussing with bags, ready to get off."

"I waited. I heard the normal two bursts on the horn showing we were leaving, and then nothing. We didn't move. After a minute or two, I looked out the door, up to the front. Nothing. I noticed someone going up the road behind the station towards the parking lot."

"What did they look like?" Donovan made notes.

"I couldn't see anything but a dark outline. He limped through. I remember that."

More notes.

"Was it a man?"

"I couldn't tell. I got off and started to the front to see what was up with Blatchford, but by the time I reached the baggage car, I could see the engine had gone without us. Something was wrong. That couldn't happen by accident, and even if it did, the engineer would know right away. I ran to the station to call down. I could hear the RS3 crossing the bridge. The crash happened while I was talking to Jenkins at the Goderich station. He swore. I could hear the engine roar by and then the sound of the crash over the phone. A few seconds later, I could hear the wreck without the phone."

"The passengers were getting feisty, but I couldn't tell them anything. I tried calling back and about forty-five minutes later, got Jenkins on the phone. He said Blatchford was dead, Jones was missing, and he would send Harry in the switcher to bring the train down to the station. It was a mess down there, and right away, 6275 brought us back to Maitland, where we spent the night. I think that's all."

"The Goderich police didn't interview you?"

"I never saw them. They were probably in way over their heads."

"I'll look this over and talk to the others. I may have more questions. Thanks Harold."

"The best place to talk to this crew is at Maitland. They overnight there. Millie's is an excellent hotel, clean anyway and has good food. You might stay there."

When train 100 reached Maitland, they held it waiting for orders. The new plan was to send it all the way to Goderich. There had been no attempt to move the RS3 or coach, but the crane blocked the station while the track crew replaced the second lead switch.

Everyone got off and wandered around the station. A few passengers made free calls on Ed's phone to have someone pick them up at Maitland. Donovan wondered if he had time to register at the hotel.

"Can I carry that for you?" Chuck Bisco limped up to Donovan and held out his hand.

"Can you make the hotel?" Mike looked at Chuck's leg.

"For two bits, I would try running there." Bisco grinned.

"Here's a quarter, but let's just walk and talk."

Chuck seized the suitcase. Mike carried the battered satchel.

"Tell me about Maitland Station." Donovan was thinking about Harold's comment that Blatchford had been fighting with people here. As a cop, Donovan was suspicious until convinced otherwise.

"It's a two bit town," Chuck laughed, making fun of his own fee. "Millie and Kat are nice, so are a lot of the others. Some are mean and crooked, too."

"Who are Millie and Kat?"

"Millie owns the hotel. She'll be at the desk when we get there. Kat, Kathleen is her daughter." Chuck sounded wistful. Donovan noticed.

"Nice Irish name, same as my grandmother." Donovan took out a handkerchief. Mopping his brow revealed his own greying red hair.

"Millie ain't Irish, but I think Kat's father is, though no one's talking. I heard."

"Heard what?"

"Mr. O'Connell, he runs the steam engine. I heard he's the father."

"So, O'Connell and Millie...?"

"Yup, it's strange. She's nice. Al isn't." For the first time, Donovan saw a frown on Chuck's face.

The detective stopped in the middle of the street to think. So far, he had only talked to two people and already they suggested this might be more complicated than he had thought. As his Irish Grandmother had been fond of saying, "there are shenanigans afoot".

"Hey, come on," Chuck grabbed his arm. "Get off the street. We don't enjoy getting our visitors run over, at least not until we know them."

Millie turned out to be a good-looking woman on the top side of forty. She had soft dark eyes. Her last name was 'French', and she looked it.

An hour later, with everyone back on board, train 100 slid into Goderich station. They had left the grain cars at Maitland. O'Connell would have to steam back to retrieve them.

"Blatchford's dying has caused us a lot more work." Al laughed. The crash had eliminated his genuine worry.

Down the track, Donovan could see the mangled wreck. A track crew was repairing the rails between the recovered lead switch and the remains of 8439. Once they laid a new track for the crane, they would recover the diesel. Mike wanted to inspect it before it moved. Donovan pulled his jacked cuffs down, straightened his tie, and went inside. Stationmaster Jenkins was in his office with Goderich Police Chief Bowers.

"Can I interrupt?" Mike walked in without waiting for an answer. "I'm Michael Donovan, Special Constable of the CSR." He handed each man a card.

Bowers was a tall, slender man in an ill-fitting uniform. His eyes were dark and calm and watching Donovan. Mike decided the man was intelligent.

The two locals accompanied Mike to the RS3. It was on its side, and there was no easy way to get to the exposed fireman's doorway. Jenkins went to arrange for a ladder.

Donovan hung his jacket and hat on the knuckle-pin lever.

"What's that?" Mike pointed at a bit of board tied to the handle with baling wire. He looked carefully and saw that it held the locking-pin by the jamming the lever. "That's strange. It looks deliberate."

The ladder arrived. Donovan opened his case and removed some thin leather work-gloves. They were clean. He was not a worker. Bowers glance into the case and saw a holster with a snub-nosed revolver.

"I see you pack some heat." Bowers had heard the expression from his hero, Broderick Crawford, on the Wingham television show, 'Highway Patrol'.

"Not much heat," Donovan chuckled as he closed the case. "That thing might scare the ignorant or do some damage at ten feet. We used the long barrel and heavier load in the RCMP." Mike was modest. He could have good accuracy at a considerable distance. The Chief had a buster brown and holster with a light, long barrel .38. It did not look as if the weapon had ever been out of the holster.

"I haven't looked inside," Bowers said as Mike climbed. "The firefighters described it, and since it's an accident, I didn't see the need."

"So, you think it was accidental?" Donovan glanced back as he twisted under the handrail and stood on the side of the remains of the short-hood. The door was hanging open against the steel sheet metal of the short cowling, as the firefighters had left it after extracting Blatchford's body. Bowers reached the hood as Donovan peered through the doorway and shone his flashlight into the gloom. It was now about an hour before sunset, twenty-two hours after a man had died in here. Mike was momentarily quiet, respecting someone he had never met.

"Quite a mess," he finally said. "Did the firefighters take anything out other than Blatchford's body?"

"Nothing. No one's been in here since then."

Donovan heaved his body over the hinge frame, with his feet finding some solid purchase. Gradually, he worked his way to the engineers' inside wall, which was now a sloping floor. Bowers peered in silently.

"I'll need to talk to everyone who was in here. I want to be sure they touched nothing."

"No problem there," said Bowers, peering in from the doorway. "None of them stayed any longer than necessary. Two of them threw up once the body was outside. It was gruesome. I'll get the names."

Donovan saw the drag marks where the men handled the body. He could see where Blatchford had pitched forward and hit the front bulkhead past the control console. There was a lot of blood on the cabin floor, which was now the far wall but little in the corner or window frame where the crumpled body ended up after the wrecked engine came to rest. There was something strange about the blood on the floor. The forward window had shattered. Glass and dirt had poured in. A little toad, probably scooped up by the shattered window, hopped near his foot and startled Donovan. Mike picked it up and handed the creature to the skeptical Bowers.

"Set this little gaffer outside. There have been enough casualties. He'll have a good story to tell the tadpoles."

"Do toads have tadpoles?" Bowers had never thought about it. He placed the little animal at the low end of the wreck. It would have to find its own way to the ground.

"There's not much blood up there." Donovan edged towards the corner. "Maybe it's under this debris." He moved the dirt away. He had already sacrificed his shoe-shine; his clean gloves now joined them.

"What's this?" Donovan extracted a large wrench. His mental reconstruction suggested the body must have been on top of the tool. The force of the dirt coming through the window had pushed them inwards. He paused, staring at the heavy forging. It didn't seem out of place in a diesel cab. He shone his light along its length. The CSR steam shop had stamped its logo into the metal. They had nothing to do with maintaining the RS3. There appeared to be blood and hair on the big end.

Blatchford must have slammed into this, or vice versa, during the crash.

It was the obvious idea. Donovan did not like the obvious. He handed the thing up to Bowers.

"Don't mess it up. Put on some gloves. Get a clean bag. I want this thing checked."

Mike slowly panned his flashlight over the complete interior, finally returning to the blood on the wall.

Footprints!

Donovan finally emerged from the wreck. His white shirt had smudged and his gloves were dirty. He held a tattered notebook, Blatchford's personal log, along with a bloody ball cap.

"That was interesting." He watched Bowers deposit the big wrench into a new mail bag. "Wait for a minute. I want a picture." Mike pulled a small Kodak camera from his satchel and snapped a few photographs of the wrench lying on the canvas bag. "I hope there are prints on that thing. Ask them to check the stuff that looks like blood and hair. This cap too," he handed the baseball cap over. "It must have still been on his head when he took the blow."

"Get them to dust this wood for prints, too. Not much chance, but who knows?" Mike snapped a few photos of the jammed handle and the knuckle. "I know a bit about trains. My Dad worked for the CNR in Orillia. I saw no one tie off a knuckle release handle."

"I'll have to call the OPP," Bowers was apologetic. "We're just a hick force here."

"I'm sure you do a great job." Donovan wanted Bowers to be a help, not a foe. If nothing else, local authorities knew all the gossip.

"I used to police a small town, too. Usually, we just had to deal with Saturday night drunks and barking dogs. There wasn't much support either."

The men laughed together. In fact, Donovan had policed a small outpost deep in the Canadian north as the lone Mountie. His problems had been much graver and led to his eventual retirement from the RCMP.

"The throttle was in the fifth notch and no one had applied the brakes." Donovan seemed to talk to himself. "Blatchford never even tried to stop."

"What's that mean?" Bowers asked.

"Two possibilities," Donovan said. "Either it was suicide or Blatchford was already unconscious, maybe dead, before the crash. If it was suicide, though, why didn't he have the throttle full on at the eighth notch? When will the autopsy be done?"

"What autopsy?" Bowers asked, suddenly embarrassed. "We figured it was an accident. The body's still up at the hospital, though."

"Get the body examined. I would like a full report."

"Who's paying?" Money was always a constraint in the small town. Some Councillors were even trying to freeze Bower's pay, as if two thousand a year was too much. They would not replace the old 1953 Ford cruiser with its oil leak and front-end rattle.

"Bill the CSR," Donovan smiled.

No doubt the lawyers would argue, and Webster would yell at him. His Mountie experience told him this thing smelled. Bowers had no experience with big crime and needed his help.

"I have to go back in and take some pictures. There are footprints in the blood on the original cab floor."

"What does that mean?"

"Unless your firefighters walk sideways, I'd say someone walked in the blood after Blatchford bled there. I'll get a blood sample from there and the window frame."

Mike was back beside Bowers as the darkening shadows hid the ground. He packed up his briefcase and frowned at the smudges on his shirt.

"I want to talk to Jones."

"What's he doing down there?" O'Connell stood with Jenkins on the station platform, watching Donovan and Bowers scrambling around the dead diesel.

"Do they think it was murder?" Albert sounded worried. He removed his stripped cap, wiped his brow, and jammed it back onto his head.

"Well, a guy dies and hundreds of thousands in CSR property destroyed. Donovan has to do a report to tie it all up." Jenkins was more concerned about getting his little empire back to normal. The road-master's caboose sat on the stub near the bunkhouse. He did not like having higher managers hanging around.

"Do you think it was murder?" Jenkins glanced at Al.

"No, no," Al said hurriedly. "I just thought it strange, that's all. I have to bring the empties up to Maitland and down tomorrow for 101."

O'Connell hurried towards the waiting Pacific. Bower's patrol car left in a cloud of dust and flying gravel, taking Donovan up the hill to the hospital.

"You don't think it was an accident?"

Bowers sounded disappointed. He was visualizing a pile of paper and long hours. It was actual police work and interesting, something beyond dog catching and sobering up farm boys and salt miners on Saturday night.

"It doesn't add up that way for me." Donovan grabbed the frame of the draft window as Bowers bounced the patrol car through the CNR yard, past the grain elevators and onto the poorly levelled gravel of North Harbour Road. "You should get some of those new fangled seat-belts."

"Council would never pay for them, and I usually take the other street up by the lighthouse. It's smoother, tar and stone. Someone reported a stray dog down here, so I thought I'd kill two birds with one stone." Bowers frowned at the memory of the actual killing.

"Up north, the Cree used to say that if your dog ran away, it was commenting on your character."

Mike smiled. He could not remember ever getting a lost dog report.

"The way they set the controls," Donovan continued, "Blatchford either committed suicide or was unconscious before the wreck. The lack of blood where the body landed says Blatchford was dead before his body hit against the front window. Most of the blood was on the engine floor, as if he had died there and bled out a bit."

"I think it was suicide then, if it wasn't an accident." Bowers slowed and frowned at a stump that looked like his stray dog in the late evening shadows.

"It's a complicated way to kill oneself, although it would explain the uncoupling from the train. Was there a bullet hole or stab wounds? Where's the gun or knife? What's the motive?" Donovan was more bothered than ever. "Those tracks in the blood are another thing. The throttle was only in the fifth notch. A suicide would have been more certain at full speed."

"Jones is in awful shape. Maybe they had a fight, and Blatchford thought he had killed Jones and dumped him at Meneset. Then he got remorse and killed himself."

"Still, it's a strange way to commit suicide. Why didn't he jump off the bridge, or use a gun out in the trees? If that's how it happened, then the blood on the floor had to be Jones' blood. Let's see what Jones says."

"You can't go in there. He's too hurt," the nurse glared at the two cops. "Doc says he has a concussion."

"We only want to ask a couple of quick questions." Donovan smiled.

"No!"

"Now Jane," Bowers leaned on the elevated desk surrounding the nurse's domain, "I remember letting your Gary off the time he took that bike. Maybe you owe me one." Bowers had been careful not to use the word, 'steal'. On her meagre nurse's salary, Jane struggled to raise her son. She had a lot of pride.

"I remember," she said.

Bowers could not resist telling the whole story. Perhaps he thought the big shot detective would think he was a poor cop for letting a crook off.

"He told me he wanted to be a doctor like his mom," Bowers chuckled and winked at the nurse. "He'll get that sorted out later. Meantime, I told him his punishment was that if he ever became a big time doctor with a big pay cheque, he had to buy a new bike every year for some poor kid who couldn't have one. He promised. You hold him to it, Jane."

"Five minutes," she nodded towards the darkened hallway and led the two to Jones' room.

"I can't remember anything." Jones was groggy, high on morphine with his head covered in bandage. A sling immobilized his strained left shoulder. The charge nurse hovered near the doorway, ready to pounce.

"Why can't you remember?" Donovan was tired and wanted answers. He forgot to be polite.

"Why do you think?" Jones used his free right hand to point at his head. "It sounds like a dozen engine bells clanging in there." Jane frowned and moved to the middle of the room. Donovan knew he had to baby Jones.

"I remember coming to, cold and hurting, against a tree. That's a steep bank between the track and the river."

"He was about thirty feet down wedged against an oak tree," said Bowers. "He must have hit hard."

"I think I remember the ride to Meneset," Jones' speech slurred. "It was a beauty of a sunset last night. I think I can remember the stop at the station, but then it's a blank. Someone clobbered me."

"Are you sure? Did you see someone?"

"No, at least I don't remember anyone, but how else could it have happened?"

"Did you fight with Blatchford?"

"Bill? No. He wasn't my favourite guy, but I only rode with him a few times a week. We didn't mix. He was going to get a mainline job and..." Jones seemed to fall asleep. His head slumped to one side and his eyes closed. The nurse checked his pulse and ushered the cops from the room.

Donovan paused. "Are Mr. Jones clothes here?"

"In the little cupboard," the nurse nodded towards the corner. She was more concerned with her patient than his belongings.

Donovan examined the contents. The left shoulder of Jones' shirt was bloody. The shirt torn and dirty as were the pants. Mike felt through all the pockets and examined the boots.

"Have they have cleaned these things at all?"

"No," she said. "This is a hospital, not a laundry." Everyone chuckled.

"How did he get hurt?"

"He has a gash and a nasty bruise on the left side of his head." Jane nodded towards the door.

Mike and Bowers quietly left the room with the worried nurse watching Jones' face intently.

"Do you have coloured pictures of the body and wreck, and I want to see Blatchford's clothes and boots?" Donovan asked as they reached the car.

"I can get them for you. My report too." Bowers was about to drive to the police station.

"I'll look at that stuff tomorrow. I need to talk to Jones again when he's in better shape, see what he knows about that wrench. There was no blood on his boots and the tread was wrong. The blood on his left shoulder suggests he either landed on his head falling from the train, or our mysterious right-handed person clobbered him, too. It looks to me from his pants that he landed hard on his ass instead and slid down the hill. The seat of his pants is full of mud, leaves and twigs, but not much elsewhere."

"So he might have fallen that way, or jumped and made sure his back end took the fall." Bowers paused at the town's traffic light.

"Yup, one or the other," Donovan yawned. "Can you do me a favour and run me up to the hotel in Maitland Station?" Donovan yawned again.

Chapter Seven

Donovan sat on a bench on the platform at Maitland station, beneath an electric light that was just now being challenged by the strengthening dawn. He could see the Pacific on the engine shed track, steamed up. Three men were checking out the beast before the workday began. One was O'Connell. Mike assumed another was the fireman. The man fooling with the tender coupling would be the frontend brakeman. The eastern sky was brightening. Crows were arguing on the far side of the road in the little wooded park beside the creek. Donovan pulled Blatchford's tattered notebook from his briefcase.

The journal wasn't a diary, but it wasn't an official CSR issued logbook either. Blatchford kept random notes and observations, meandering from complaints about his wife to mundane details of a particular run, especially if something out of the ordinary had happened. There were some occasional unflattering descriptions of various railway managers. Donovan leafed through the pages looking for names. He wanted to know if Blatchford had a hate on for anyone, or if he mentioned anyone who might not like him.

O'Connell's name stood out with the note. *Crazy old-fashioned bastard.* There was no threat either way. Nearing the end of the record, there was an entry printed at the top of a page, a *strange boxcar at Mile 47, on cattle siding.* Below the entry he had added, *car number 315387, must check into it.* And then below that, *went to see train man in Guelph, not a number for a boxcar.* There were dates on each entry. Several pages went by with unimportant entries and then, *no records in the Maitland manifests,* below that, *saw 315387 at the factory by the mill, threatened by the factory jerk, he pulled a gun on me that night at the station, tried to blackmail me. I took his gun.* He saw the curt phrase, *"Millie's a bitch"* dated *the next day.* There were a few more unrelated notes. The journal was blank after that.

What did Blatchford find? Who's the jerk? Why was Millie a bitch? Donovan liked the hotel owner.

The bell on locomotive 1232 clanged. Al gave two short toots on his way to arrange the freight cars to hitch to 101 on the run to Guelph.

It was just after six. The sky was much brighter. Ed walked through the parking lot past his Buick, retrieved the key from behind the brick, and unlocked the station door. Donovan followed him into the office.

"Too drunk to drive home last night?" Donovan joked.

Ed flared, but then realized Mike was not serious.

"Nope, I leave the car here most of the time. It actually belongs to the CSR. I only drive home for lunch, or if we have to go shopping. It's always with me on the weekend. We like to go over to Port Albert in the summer for a picnic and a swim."

Ed frowned, thinking perhaps Donovan would not approve of his personal use of company property. He needn't have worried. Mike drove his railway cop car to the A & P and anywhere else he wanted. Byng Webster did not know about that. They always paid the gas chits with no question. No doubt Byng Webster had his own little scam.

"Have you ever come across this car?" Donovan stepped towards Ed's desk, fishing for Blatchford's notebook. He nearly tripped over a box of tools, smudging his grey slacks. "Damn!"

"Oh, that's those old steam tools. I forgot to get them to the engine shed. Sorry about that."

Mike repeated the boxcar number.

"It's a strange number," Ed frowned. "No CSR boxcar has that number, I don't think."

Mike remembered Blatchford's reference to a jerk at the factory and seeing the boxcar on their siding.

"Could the furniture factory own that boxcar?" There were many private dedicated cars all over Canada.

Ed was trying to decide how to avoid Donovan's question. It shook him that somehow this cop knew about the boxcar and had already connected it to the factory. Chuck Bisco limped in.

"Hey Chuck," Ed seized the chance to delay, hoping Donovan would forget the boxcar. "Can you take this box of tools over to the engine shed? Yell at those kids over there playing on the coal crib, too. Send them off. I don't want some mother coming in here complaining that I let their kid get covered in coal dust or get a scraped knee or something."

Mike watched Bisco limp away with the heavy box on a two wheeled hand cart.

"He's mobile," said Donovan, "even though he's struggling."

"Chuck's a gamer," Ed made a show of searching for some paperwork. "He even owns a car, drives all over."

"You don't say." Donovan made some notes in his book.

Chuck limps.

"You never saw that boxcar?"

"Nope, it shouldn't have passed through this yard without being on a manifest. Maybe it's in Guelph."

"Maybe," Donovan mused, looking through the window towards the spur that ran up to the furniture factory.

"I've got to gas up the Buick," Ed eagerly changed the subject. "It seemed to be down a lot yesterday. I rarely let it get this low. Can you sit here for ten while I run up to the Supertest?" He retrieved his car keys from the desk drawer and disappeared.

***

Chuck Bisco struggled across the yard. The two wheeled handcart was not heavy, but his lame leg made it awkward. He had to pick his way, using the walkways with their planks between the tracks. It doubled the length of his ordeal. He would never refuse a job like this. He would never let his leg defeat him.

"Hey, you two," Chuck called up to the boys, enjoying the sound and feel of the lumps of coal grinding beneath their feet as they scampered about on top of the coal hopper. They were ten years old and lived just over from Chuck.

"Ed can see you over here. I told you before, you got to be smart and stay out of sight. Hey, did you check out that coal car over on the stub? Throwing the leftovers around in them is fun, but make sure there's enough coal to let you climb back out."

Chuck remembered the one time it had trapped him in an open gondola car. It was a different stationmaster then, and he had caught whatfor. The man yelling at him was nothing. It was the bum warming he got from his mother later that hurt the most. After that, he only played in the cars with bigger boys who could help him get out. Chuck decided if he ever had kids, he would never spank them but throw coal with them, or maybe not.

"The old engine in the shed is fun, too. Just take nothing."

Chuck waved and moved on to deposit his load in the unused third bay of the engine shed. Bisco did not think about how his efforts with the children had been the opposite of what Ed had asked him to do. No one had ever come close to dying when he was a kid, and the yard had been much busier back then.

Chuck limped into the station and put a coffee percolator on the hotplate. Donovan waited on a passenger bench.

Maybe they all did it, a grand conspiracy. He smiled to himself. The beginning of an investigation was always confusing.

"Want a coffee, Mr. Donovan?" Chuck was holding two heavy China CSR mugs, the ones with the picture of an old steam locomotive crossing a high trestle.

"Sure, thanks," Mike frowned.

"Cream and sugar?"

"Black thanks. When I was up north, it was too much trouble to fly all that in. I would rather have my tobacco."

As if to emphasize the point, Donovan pulled his pipe from the jacket pocket, stuffed it with Amphora Brown, and lit it with a military style lighter.

Chuck sat beside Mike. He seemed to need a friend.

"I never smoked. I couldn't afford it. Mom wouldn't approve."

"How'd you hurt your leg?" Mike blew on the coffee and sipped. Chuck brewed it strong.

"Mother says the doctor yanked on my leg too hard. I was being born breach, you know, legs first instead of my head." He laughed. "I never enjoy diving into water head first. I guess I was born that way."

Chuck's laugh was infectious. Donovan, behind his chuckling, was trying to decide on an easy way to ask the hard questions. He sucked on his pipe and made a show of relighting it.

"You seem to be smart enough."

"I graduated high school, good marks too. The doc pulled my leg; he didn't drop me on my head," more laughter. Mike liked this young man.

Still, he limps. Donovan thought.

"Did you know Blatchford?"

Chuck frowned. "He wasn't a nice man, at least not to me. He always poked fun at my leg, but not joking either. I avoided him if I could. He was after Kat, Kathleen, Millie's daughter."

"I like her. I think they did, you know," Chuck blushed and flashed a fleeting angry look.

Donovan shifted uncomfortably. As a cop, he wanted to know everything, and this was useful. As a human, it was too much information.

Motive...

"Then Millie found out Blatchford was married and ran him off. The bar manager told me she hit him with a heavy curtain rod." Bisco grinned. "I think if it had been a sword, she would have killed him. Kat might have too. She was pretty mad, and sad." Chuck looked sad too.

"Blatchford went and killed himself first and robbed them of all the satisfaction. I would have killed him too, if Kat had asked me."

"That's strong language, Chuck. You should not talk like that. I'm investigating the crash, but I'm not sure it was an accident or suicide."

Chuck looked startled. "I... I wouldn't really kill anyone. Believe me." He looked scared.

Donovan smiled reassuringly. He wanted Chuck to be at ease. Deep down, he wanted Bisco to be innocent.

"I never accused you. Tell me about the night before last, up here. If there is something funny about Blatchford's death, it must connect to here. My impression is no one in Goderich hated him."

"I saw nothing. I had dinner with Mom and then went to the movie in Goderich. The Bob Hope movie 'Alias Jesse James' is on this week. Hope is funny.

"I stopped to see if Kathleen wanted to come, but her mother said Kat was not well," Chuck relaxed, "so I saw nothing around here. The movie lasted from seven until about nine. When I got back here about half an hour later, the place was like a tomb," Chuck frowned. "I guess that was a bad thing to say since a guy died."

"Works for me," laughed Donovan. "He wasn't nice to you, and I didn't know the guy. You didn't see anyone else?"

"I saw Al O'Connell come into town from that way," he pointed north. "He was driving Millie's car and tore into the hotel lot, fast. He even skidded a bit. Al and Millie have been sleeping together for a long time. He takes her car sometimes. I paid little attention and went home."

"What time was that?"

"Oh, about half-past nine. I was home in time to see the end of Red Skelton."

Mike made lots of notes. The incident at Meneset happened just after eight, the crash about twenty minutes later. Timing seemed important. Chuck only had Bob Hope as a rather poor alibi, backed up by the even more doubtful Freddie the Free Loader.

Opportunity...

"Have you ever been in a diesel locomotive?"

"Not with Blatchford, that's damned sure. When Ed ran that older diesel, he used to let me ride with him to Goderich, when I was a kid. It was fun, a big thrill. Diesels were the new thing replacing the old-fashioned steam engines." Chuck paused, smiling at some of the best memories of his childhood. "Sometimes we were down there for hours. I got to ride 6275 a bit too and see the big ships come in. It all ended when Ed got the job running things here."

"One more thing," Chuck seemed eager, perhaps sensing he was not above suspicion. "Kat is Al's daughter. I overheard Millie and Al talking once. That's how I found out Blatchford was fooling around with Kat. I overheard that jerk Winslow from the factory trying to embarrass Millie."

"I guess that would have made O'Connell angry with Blatchford."

"Oh, he already hated him. He threatened to get Blatchford once, here in the station, over moving the freight cars. If Blatchford was after Kat, I guess Al would have been even madder."

"Could Al kill Blatchford?" Mike thought the question unfair, but wanted to see Chuck's reaction.

"I don't think so, Mr. Donovan. At least I hope not. Al's crazy wild sometimes, especially when he's drinking, but I don't think so. He didn't seem drunk when he drove that night."

"So skidding and throwing gravel about is normal for him?"

"Same as the rest of us, driving should be fun," Chuck smiled.

"Thanks, Chuck." Mike finished the coffee and relit the pipe just as Ed returned.

"I don't understand," Ed muttered as he threw the car keys into the drawer. "I put in three bucks. It's never over two-fifty. I hope Fred up there isn't shorting us at the pump. You could be sure before when the gas was in the glass. Now he has those new fangled pumps and we have to trust him. I caught Fred cheating at cards once."

"The price shot up a penny a gallon last week in Guelph." Donovan liked small talk. It would put Ed at ease if he needed more answers. "If this keeps up, we'll all be broke."

"Damned oil companies," Ed agreed. "Rockefeller getting rich on us stiffs."

"And Murray Westgate too," Chuck added. They all laughed. Then Chuck seemed to look sad. Donovan thought there might be more. What was on Chuck's mind was a surprise.

"I think my mom's dying, Mr. Donovan." The boy was near tears. "She went to the doctor last week and came home crying. I know it was bad news. She's been poorly lately. We take care of each other. I've never been on my own. She's my best friend."

"Is there anyone else you can talk to?"

"Kat and I used to talk about things, but not after Blatchford. I thought Kat would be my best friend, too. I've never been on my own." There was a sob.

"Maybe she needs a friend right now too, Chuck." Donovan was thinking if Blatchford's betrayal had hurt the girl, she would need someone, an old friend, to confide in. He had not met her and could not understand that she had attracted Chuck and Blatchford to her for different reasons, and for the same reason.

"When does the Pacific go to Goderich for the passenger train?" Mike asked Ed. "I'd like a ride."

"Any time now, I'll call Al in."

Donovan rode out of Maitland in the cabin of the Pacific.

"How well did you guys know Blatchford?" Donovan raised his voice above the sound of the locomotive. Walter and Bobby both looked at Al.

"I knew the bastard." O'Connell balled a fist. "Glad he's dead." He pulled hard on the whistle cord as they sped across the Carlow road. "I didn't kill him, if that's what you're getting at."

"I didn't mention any killing," Mike smiled.

"He was only out for himself," Walter chipped in. "Blatchford didn't care who he hurt."

"Like Millie's daughter?"

"Yah, that," Al said. "I would have killed him for that, but didn't get the chance."

"You're the second person who said that to me. I guess Blatchford had lots of enemies."

"Not me," said Walter.

"Or me," Bobby added. He turned back from the window and took off his sunglasses. "He was showing me the ropes in a diesel. I've applied for the training."

"You traitorous little bastard," Al flared. It was the first he had heard of it. He expected everyone to hate diesels as much as he did. "I take care of you and our problems, and that's the thanks I get."

"Thanks for what?" Bobby asked. "Steam's going out. I need to learn the diesel. You should thank me."

Thanks for what indeed? Donovan looked at Al and then watched Highway 21 pass beneath them.

Chief Bowers collected Donovan from Goderich station and headed up the hill to the hospital. Jones was sitting up, spooning hospital Jell-O into his mouth.

"You look better," Bowers exclaimed. "Last night you were about dead, I thought."

He's good. Donovan made a note in his book.

"Who are you guys?" Jones wiped a little Jell-O from his chin. He seemed to like the food. Railway men were not connoisseurs of five star dining.

"You don't remember? We were here last night. You talked to us." Bowers seemed annoyed. The pair of cops stood at the foot of the bed looking for the entire world as if they were about to share the good news with a hapless sinner, Bower's sidearm tagging along for extra encouragement.

"Nope, don't remember. So who are you?"

The men reintroduced themselves. Jones looked a little nervous.

"I have a few more questions," Donovan said. "There was a big wrench in the wrecked cab of the RS3. Do you know anything about it?"

"The engine... wrecked?" Jones looked surprised. "How's Bill?"

"No one told you?" Bowers glanced at Donovan and then carried on in his usual blunt, small town fashion. "He died. The engine ran past the Goderich station and crashed. It's a big mess down there."

"Damn," Jones' face broke into a strange little smile and then a frown. Mike noticed.

"Tell me about the wrench?"

"Beats me. We had no wrench in the cab. What would we need it for? We had screwdrivers and pliers and a small ball-peen hammer, flashlight, odds and sods of stuff. No big wrench. That's something you might find on a steam loco or in a repair shop. We had a big steel pry-bar if we had to bar over the engine to clear water from the pistons before starting, but that's secured under the long-hood, not in the cab."

"You never saw one on the last trip?"

"No." Jones said.

"You don't remember anyone hitting you?"

"Again... No!"

"Someone blocked the knuckle pin handle and wired it in the un-hitch position. Did you do that?"

"That's totally against the rules. I would never do that. I did coupling and uncoupling *safely*. Maybe Bill did it."

"It was on the fireman's side."

"So?" Jones was defensive. "Maybe someone wanted to be in the cab and unhitch the train without help." Jones considered the idea. "The handle needs to be held until the knuckles cleared. Still, it could have been Blatchford."

"Someone wanted only the engine to go to Goderich to protect the passengers and crew." Donovan said, writing furiously.

They asked Jones to repeat his account of the trip two nights before.

"The last I remember is Bill getting off at Meneset. There's nothing else until I was here."

"Blatchford had a notebook. He mentioned a boxcar that had him upset. Do you know about that?"

Jones grinned. "Yah, he was excited. Bill thought finding some dirt about that boxcar would get him a pat on the head and help get a main-line job. He was obsessed, figured Al O'Connell was involved in it. He and O'Connell had a hate on for each other. His poking around got everyone at Maitland Station upset. I think none of them liked him much. Millie even banned him from the hotel. He was fooling around with that pretty daughter of Millie's. He neglected to mention to Kat that he had a beautiful wife in Guelph." Jones chuckled.

"Bill had more tramps than just that girl. He was a bastard, really disrespected his wife." Jones' smile turned to a scowl. Another note for Donovan. Jones' memory stopped there.

"Barbara," Bowers and Donovan stopped the day-nurse as she hurried down the hallway, "did Jones have any other visitors?"

"A woman called from Guelph. I took it. She said where she was calling from and it was long distance, business rates too, a big spender."

"Oh, and Mr. Jenkins from the railway station came by right after breakfast."

"Do you know what they were talking about?"

"Now Richard," Barbara scolded the Chief. "You know, we aren't supposed to eavesdrop on our patents. It's against the nurses' code," she smiled.

"Did you accidentally hear anything?" Bowers winked. He knew how the gossip chain worked. This was a big deal and worth some points for the nurse at the coffee break confab.

"Well, I was checking Mr. Grieves in the next bed. Mr. Jenkins and Mr. Jones discussed the train wreck. It sounded horrible, and that man was dead and all."

"That was this morning?" Donovan asked. "Jenkins told Jones about the wreck and Mr. Blatchford being dead?"

"Yes sir." Barbara consulted the watch pinned to her smock. "About three hours ago."

The cops left.

"He made a quick recovery." Bowers turned his car towards the police station.

"That's what I was thinking. He was well enough to lie. I bet he faked not knowing who we were, maybe to convince us someone had hit him hard. Jones didn't seem to care Blatchford was dead. In whatever way this happened, someone who knew how to run diesel trains did it. Blatchford himself, or..."

"It looks like Jones is lying, but maybe the whack on the head is messing up his memory."

"Maybe..." Donovan pondered.

"We sent the body to London for the autopsy. If Blatchford didn't kill himself, that guy did it. Why else would he lie?"

"A real possibility," Mike said. "What's his motive?"

"You're the detective," Bowers laughed, "but you don't act like a big-shot cop. Maybe you're too nice a guy. You should work like I do and assume everyone is guilty and work back from there," Bowers trusted Donovan. He didn't act like a city know-it-all.

"You don't seem to be guilty," Donovan smiled. "One off my list."

In fact, Donovan assumed guilt and work backwards. Chief Bowers would be happy to know his name came off Donovan's list of suspect the night before.

"I was a cop way up north, surrounded by people everyone wrote off as drunken Indians. Some were in awful shape, but a lot of them taught me not to judge people too quickly or reach conclusions too soon before pulling out the gun and the cuffs. Some, many, showed me how to hunt and fish and trap, works for two-legged prey too."

"If Jones has a motive, it must have something to do with Guelph." Bowers parked in the square opposite the police station.

"Richard, my friend, you have some brilliant insight. Do the OPP have the wrench and wood to check?"

"They sure do."

"Have Blatchford's boots checked for blood and get me a picture of the tread?"

"I'll buy you lunch. Where can I get this film developed?"

13

Chapter Eight

Bowers and Donovan parted outside the café. The Chief went off to check out a complaint of a teenager smoking in the alley behind the Hexagon Hotel. This late in the summer, just before school reopened, the bored kids were his biggest problem.

Donovan crossed the circular road and sat on a bench beneath the statue of a World War One soldier. Mike thought over what he knew so far and pondered his next move. It looked like he needed to beg a ride back to Maitland Station.

"Hello, Mr. Donovan," Chuck's greeting startled Mike.

"Hi, Chuck, who's this nice young lady?" Donovan raised his tweed fedora high in greeting. The girl was beautiful.

"I'm Kathleen, Mr. Donovan," she giggled. "When you raised your hat, you looked like that tin man behind you."

Donovan twisted on the bench and looked at the memorial. The statue of a World War One soldier raised his flack helmet in salute.

"He has more right to raise his hat than I do. Do you see the thousands behind him?"

Chuck and Kat frowned, not understanding Donovan's reference to sacrifice. Mike thought of the one Remembrance Day when he had stood in the rain, shivering in his red surge, water dripping from the brim of his Stetson and thinking, *at least I'm not knee deep in muck and I won't have to duck bullets.*

He remembered the many older men in the crowd, grim faced, splendid in their Legion dress, staunchly suffering in the rain, flinching at the sound of the gun salute. Donovan could never share their horror.

"Are you heading back to Maitland soon?" Mike returned to the present warm day.

"We'll give you a ride." Kathleen volunteered Chuck's car. The three headed off, with Chuck squealing tires as they pulled into the street.

"That'll get someone complaining to Bowers," Chuck laughed.

"Does everyone drive like that around here?"

"If you want to be hip," Kat giggled.

"Hip?" Donvan asked. "Where the hell to your young ones get that talk?"

"Radio, CKLW," Chuck said.

Donovan learned two things on the drive. Chuck loved Kathleen, and Kathleen knew it. It wasn't clear how much affection she had for the young man. Donovan was no expert, but he thought a woman betrayed may not find it easy to trust again.

All of this saddened Mike. He had not written off anyone as a suspect, and Chuck's love and his knowledge of Blatchford's seduction and deception of Kat could be motive enough.

Damn it, he thought, *I like the boy.*

He still followed Police Chief Bower's dictum and suspected most people until he could check them off his suspect list. He had been teasing Bowers. Jenkins was off the list, too. He could not be in two places at once.

What I need to do is find the one who seems to have been in two places at once, but wasn't.

As they entered Millie's dining room, Donovan tried to summarize his case. He had convinced himself there had been a murder, and the wrench was the murder weapon. The OPP tests would prove it and maybe provide the killer's fingerprints. His most likely suspect, Jones, did not seem to have a motive, and the way events unfolded, he would have needed an accomplice. There were too many others with motives.

As he sat, he added up the questions. Perhaps those footprints in the blood would help, and for sure the blood would prove to be Blatchford's, unless the blood was on Blatchford's boots. Once he had his photographs, he could look for dusty spots where his suspects would have left tracks.

He ordered a beer.

Who knew how to run the diesel, had a motive and had the opportunity? Who did it?

Mike wasn't sure he had the first three lists complete. Maybe he was barking up the wrong tree and some enemy of Blatchford's from Guelph or elsewhere killed him. Maybe Blatchford had a married lover whose husband killed him. He knew that once he had filled all the categories, an arrow would run through a name on the three lists to answer the last question. The wrench, maybe with other evidence, would be the arrow.

Kathleen, now in her work apron, placed a glass of beer in front of Mike. She sat.

"I'm glad he's dead," Kat blurted out. "I thought I loved him. Now I hate him."

"Hated him enough to kill him?" Donovan had decided the answer was 'no', whatever the girl said. If her relationship with Blatchford had lasted longer, she might have learned how to run a diesel locomotive. As it was, Donovan doubted she even knew how to ring its bell.

"I don't know," she answered honestly, then burst into tears. "I feel humiliated."

"Your first love usually tears your heart to bits," Mike thought back to high school. He thought of Chuck, smitten by this fine looking and smart, red-head. He now saw how Blatchford, in his lustful indifference, could want this pretty young woman.

"Chuck wants to help."

Kathleen kept sobbing with her face in her hands. Donovan did not play the honest cupid. He wanted to have more opportunity to see the two youngsters together. Mike needed to know what Chuck was capable of. Otherwise, his Irish heart made him a matchmaker.

Grandmother would be proud of me. Donovan smiled.

Millie had been watching from the kitchen doorway. She hurried over and placed a protective hand on her daughter's shoulder.

"Kathleen," she said gently, "go into the kitchen and have a nice cup of tea. I want to talk to Mr. Donovan."

Kat stood. Millie sat.

"She's very sad," Mike stated the obvious, trying to avoid any scolding from Millie.

"She is, Mr. Donovan..."

"Call me Mike. Mister was my father."

"That bastard used her. I'm glad he's dead, too. Does that make me a suspect?"

"You think someone murdered him?"

"Al thinks so. He said he hoped so and hopes Blatchford suffered. He hated him for a lot of reasons to do with the railway. Kathleen was the last straw."

"Why would he hate him for what Blatchford did to Kathleen?"

"Mike, Albert is her father." Millie was not embarrassed, and long ago learned to ignore judgmental people, if that was his reaction. She did not know this was old news to Donovan. She did not know Donovan.

Maybe he's just another son of an Irishman like Al. Millie thought.

"Al was furious, but he scared me when he found out about Kat and Blatchford. Normally, he would shout and rant and throw things. He's Irish, you know." Millie blushed at the Irish cop. "Oh, I'm sorry."

"But right," said Mike. "It wasn't my dad, though. My mother and grandmother, Dad's mother, would... well... you know. But they never actually duked it out," he added hastily.

"He just sat quietly," Millie continued, "when I told him Blatchford was already married. Al said Blatchford would pay for it or something like that and didn't act at all like himself. I guess we're all suspects," she smiled at Donovan.

He's cute for a railway cop, another Irishman. I wonder if he's married.

"You all have motives," Mike smiled back. "You and Kathleen are way down the list, on two counts. Neither of you have a clue how to run a diesel like the RS3. Second, the killer, if there was a killer, other than the fireman Jones, had to drive to Meneset. Kat has no car. Al had your car, so you had no way of getting there. I'm sure I would find lots of witnesses to say you were both here all that evening."

"You would," Millie seemed relieved and surprised.

"How did you know Al had my car? Does that make him a suspect?"

"Someone saw him."

"I guess Al's a suspect then."

"Second from the top," Donovan did not smile. He thought Millie loved Al.

"I hope he didn't do it," Millie said, "but it wouldn't surprise me or sadden me if he did. He has that big temper I mentioned."

Mike raised his eyebrows. Millie was not defending O'Connell. He would make a note later.

"I'm done with Al," Millie continued without prompting. "He's only found me comfortable and never even admitted he had a daughter until a guy he already didn't like messed around with her. He's way older than me. Don't tell him, but he's going to be gone soon."

It was not clear to Mike if she was making an argument for throwing Al out of her life, or telling Donovan she was more his age and might soon be available. Mike suddenly felt as if he was back north, stalking game through the black spruce, afraid to step on a dry twig that might betray him.

Careful...

"Am I a wicked woman, a terrible mother?"

"Of all the women I've met, you're near the saintly end of the list. My old grandmother used to say, 'we're all sinners. Some just have more fun at it.' She was a regular at Mass, too. My grandfather died young. I shudder to think what the Priest heard in the confessional. She would have told the old priest too, paid her dollar, said her hail-Mary's and carried on with her life."

Mike chuckled. Millie smiled.

Donovan lingered alone at Millie's table through dinner, tossing the problem around in his mind. Once the rush subsided, Millie returned carrying a small bottle of red wine and two glasses.

"Celebrating?" asked Donovan.

"Just welcoming a handsome guest."

In his imagination, Mike's foot hovered above a dry twig. He hoped it was not a bear trap.

Millie poured the wine and peeked over the bottle at Mike.

"My favourite brand," Donovan said.

"This kind," Millie looked at the label, "Spanish Yago?"

"The free kind," Donovan laughed. "He had already downed three beers."

"How did you end up in this hotel?" Mike knew most people wouldn't have the money for this kind of business.

"I was married once," Millie sipped wine and looked sad, "before the war. He went into the navy and died." She didn't volunteer more.

"I'm sorry," said Donovan.

"Me too," she whispered.

"We had always talked of running a hotel. There was a little government payment, not much, and I had saved some from working over at the air training base in Goderich. The down payment wasn't much and the old owner took the mortgage. He wanted to retire. It's paid off now." Millie sounded proud. "It used to be busier, but everything's declining."

Donovan did some math. There was more to the story. Kat must have been born before the war ended.

The Pacific steamed through, fronting train 100. The whistle as it crossed Main Street reverberated through the room.

"Al will be here about half-past nine," Millie frowned. "What about you, Donovan? How did you become a railway dick?"

"Dick? You watch too many Bogart movies. I joined the Mounties before the war. It finally got to me."

"What, you were tired of escorting the Queen and The Chief?" Millie laughed. The Royal Tour had just wrapped up. She did not like the Prime Minister, 'Dief the Chief'. The pomp and circumstance had come nowhere near Maitland Station. Stratford was the closest.

"No," Mike joined the laughter, "I spent my whole career way up north, almost to the tundra, isolated as hell."

"I guess Mrs. Donovan wouldn't like that." Millie was hopeful.

"There's no Mrs. Donovan." Mike frowned, imagining a twig snapping or a trap closing, slowly. "You could never expect a woman to live that far out. There were native women, but it did not tempt me. Some guys did and left some women high and dry with kids. The force always got them out before the town lynched them."

"Seriously?"

"No, but they were useless after doing that. They lost all their authority and had to be replaced. Unless some officer liked them, they usually went to a worse place as punishment. I grew to like the folks I was involved with. I didn't want to mess it up."

"So, why did you leave?"

"The only thing I liked about the job was the people. Sure, some were drunks and others had bad problems, too much time, little hope and not much to do if you weren't out on the land. The ones who went trapping were my favourites. I think they liked me too. A lot of bad stuff went on, not all from the community but from the government. They kept carting the kids away to school, to make them white. It was sad. I put up with it until I reached a time I could muster out with a bit of pension."

"So you're a rich guy?"

"Hardly. Only the big wigs in Ottawa leave with good money, but it'll be okay when I retire. Anyway, the final straw, they ordered me to help take the kids of my closest friend. That was it. I loved those little ones." Donovan stopped, staring into the distance, and then took a deep swig of wine. Millie poured more.

Donovan likes kids. Millie thought.

"I'll tell you," Donovan leaned towards Millie and lowered his voice, "I found out ahead of time and warned them," Mike whispered, somewhat under the influence, "they took off onto the land. The Priest and the jumped up Indian Affairs social worker who flew in on the Otter were upset. I tried not to laugh. They wanted to take them to Fort Chipewyan. I resigned right after and got out before winter. Probably, when my replacement had the job, those kids got nabbed anyway. I hope not. At least it wasn't me. It's a horrible thing."

Millie leaned forward so that her forehead pressed against Donovan's, her bright red painted lips an inch from his. They looked conspiratorial. Her three glasses of wine were having their effect. Her breath smelt of Spanish wine and her neck of the best Woolworth's perfume. "We all have deep, dark secrets," she whispered.

Donovan's glass was empty. He placed a hand over it when Millie tried to pour.

"I've talked too much, too much wine as it is. You're plying me with liquor. It's supposed to be the other way around." Mike's fuzzy brain could not stop him from snapping a twig. His quarry started, but did not flee.

"That would be nice," Millie smiled. Then she frowned again. "I have to go get the kitchen ready. Al and the crew will want supper soon."

"Can you please call me early tomorrow? I want to catch the train to Guelph."

"Are you leaving?" Millie seemed disappointed.

"No, I'll be back for dinner. I have to look for some information. Blatchford was looking into a strange boxcar. I want to find out more about it. It may have something to do with the case."

Millie gave Donovan a strange look as she left.

Guilt? Fear? His mind tried to tell him to make a note. Wine, red lips and cheap perfume said no.

Chapter Nine

Mike thought about riding in the locomotive with Al's crew, but he went in comfort, talking with Harold, the conductor in the passenger coach. Maybe another time he would ride up front and get the flavour of his suspects. He would need to dress the part. The herringbone jacket was too expensive to cover in soot. It had already suffered on the quick jaunt to Goderich in the Pacific.

"Do you know Mile 47 and the cattle siding?" Donovan asked Harold.

"We're almost on it, just the other side of Highway 23. It'll be on the left."

Mike watched through the wisps of black smoke that trailed along the train from the Pacific. Soon, the Mile 47 marker flew by along with the siding at a cattle yard. The tracks were empty.

"They ship most of the feeders in September and October," Harold said. "More slaughter cattle go to the packing houses near the end of October, just as the grass freezes off and they've had a little summer corn. There isn't much activity there otherwise. Usually, 111 lifts the cattle cars and drops empties. It's all coordinated from Guelph. They load cattle at Maitland as well."

"Did you ever see a lone boxcar there?"

"Yes, twice. I figure 111 had a hot bearing or something. If it was a bad-order, Guelph would send up a switcher to collect it and take it to the shop."

Donovan leaned over the counter in the train-master's office in Guelph. Joe had his book open.

"315387 can't be a box. Boxcars have 100 series numbers. 315387, let's see," Joe examined his book, "is a flat car on pulpwood service in Northern Ontario. It has never been to Goderich that I can tell. They cut down their trees in the last century," he laughed.

"I guess it's hard to keep track of so many cars." Donovan stared at the unending list of numbers and information for each.

"Oh, yes. Lots go missing."

"Do you have a list? Have any gone missing on the Goderich sub?"

Joe smiled. "Is grass green?"

"Do you have a list of those?"

"You ain't the first one been asking about that number. That guy Blatchford who died running the RS3, he was here about a week before he died."

"Tragic," Susan exclaimed, "he left a wife and all."

"Are you involved in that?"

Mike nodded.

"I told him he was seeing things," Joe continued, "told him just what I told you. It's running pulpwood, and then he left in a huff."

"This is interesting," Joe had flipped to the back to pages labelled, *Unaccounted For*. "Car 115387 disappeared, almost the right number. It was last manifested in Guelph, five years ago. It's a big yard. Maybe no one has looked for it, or maybe Blatchford got the number wrong." He glanced out the window at the confusing layout of tracks, spurs, and stubs of three different leads. All hosted a confusing array of rolling stock waiting for their next run.

"Why would it be on the cattle siding?"

"Beats me."

"Have you retrieved any bad-orders from there?"

"Nope, we would have to run a switcher as a special to get it. It hasn't happened. The only specials for years have been salt trains and road crews."

"If you ask me, Blatchford was a bad-order," Susan chuckled.

Donovan looked at the woman.

Is she someone Blatchford couldn't get into bed, or is she mad he didn't try?

"Did you know him well?" Mike tried to keep a poker face.

"Not *that* well," Susan chuckled again. "You have a dirty mind, Mr. Cop," she winked.

"Sorry, just doing my job."

"He was a flirt and a user. I wouldn't touch him with a ten-foot pole. Talk to his wife."

"I'll do that."

Mike left with the numbers of three missing boxcars in his book and headed down the platform to the passenger waiting room. The shoeshine boy would finally fix the scuffs that had been haunting Donovan ever since he had crawled around inside the shattered RS3. His mother would be happy. He glanced up at the big puffy clouds in a robin's egg sky.

"Please, mister."

He dropped a quarter into the little girl's basket. It clanged against some empty pop bottles.

His shirt ended up at the laundry across the street from the station and the herringbone jacket and grey pants at the dry cleaners. Mike headed home to retrieve more clothes and his spare herringbone jacket. It was likely he would be at Millie's Hotel much longer than he first expected. That was a bonus. Millie's hotel was more attractive than he expected.

***

Donovan stepped from the coach onto the Maitland Station platform. He thought, this late in the day, Chuck would not be around to earn two bits carrying his suitcase. The lights had been on in the office but went out. Chuck Bisco locked the door. Donovan watched him hide the key behind the window brick.

"Will you carry this for me?" Mike smiled. "I didn't expect to see you here."

"I wasn't stealing," Chuck said defensively. "Ed pays me to do a little cleanup twice a week. I was finishing up."

"Is that key always there?"

"Yup, Ed doesn't enjoy carrying it around in case he loses it. He keeps a spare in the car though, and a spare car key in his desk. There isn't much danger from thieves. No one local locks their doors. Locking the station is railway policy. It doesn't do much good, though. As kids, we used to get in through the express fire door. We could slip the bolt with a jackknife."

Mike wondered if Chuck had confessed all of his criminal activity so easily.

They stepped around Ed's Buick and walked across the lot. Donovan hoped Millie would feed a late arriving cop like she did her engineer.

"Have you eaten?" he asked Chuck. "I want to ask a few questions. My treat, if Millie will feed us."

Chuck and Mike ate stew. Millie kept a pot ready for late arrivals. Anyone after the dinner hour was not getting 'a la carte'.

"Have a beer on me," Donovan looked for Kat.

"No thank you, Mr. Donovan. I don't drink alcohol."

Mike raised his eyebrows. He did not want to pry.

"I boozed a lot when I was young. Once, when I came home drunk, Mom said, 'Charles, you can feel sorry for yourself and kill yourself with booze, or you can fight it. I know you feel badly about your leg, I do too. It seems it was my fault, but I pray it doesn't drag you into hell and make you a boozing bum'. She hugged me tight and cried. I love my mother. She kept me from feeling sorry for myself. I stay sober to spare her any more of it." Chuck had tears in his eyes.

"Your mother sounds like my mother," Donovan said quietly. *And his mom's dying.*

Mike ordered two Cokes.

"Chuck, the other day you called Winslow a jerk."

"Well, he is," Chuck was a little loud.

"Look here." Donovan opened Blatchford's notebook and showed Bisco the passages about the boxcar. "Blatchford referred to a 'jerk' and he said the guy pulled a gun on him outside the station. Do you think it was Winslow?"

"Once a jerk, always a jerk," Chuck laughed. "Maybe Blatchford was referring to himself." His eyes twinkled.

"Funny man," Mike put the book away.

"There is something funny going on with that boxcar," Chuck sipped. "Blatchford was on to something and was making lots of people nervous."

"I guess Winslow is in on it somehow," Chuck added.

"Tomorrow, would you drive me up to the old mill and the factory?"

Mike made a note in his own book. He had known guys like Chuck up north. He was the outsider most people never paid attention to, but he was always the guy who knew just about everything, about everyone. When someone like Chuck said, 'I guess', you could take it as a fact.

***

Chuck's Olds came to a skidding stop in the mill's sand parking lot. A cloud of dust drifted ahead, engulfing a red stake truck. The old farmer hefting sacks of barley into the mill scowled. He was about to curse out the driver when he saw Chuck ease out the driver's side.

"Damn it, Coach, if it were anyone else, I'd be giving you a hiding."

The old man, Mr. Smith, as Chuck always called him, tried not to smile. Both were fixtures of the community, and they were unlikely friends. Years before, when Chuck was still in elementary school, they often sat together on the worn wooden planks of the arena stands watching the latest glorious loss of the local junior 'B' team. It convinced the old farmer Chuck knew everything about hockey. In the winter, the arena was Chuck's home. He had watched hundreds of games, from the little tykes to the junior team, and had listened to countless coaching and practice sessions. He understood the game completely from the theory side. Smith had first called him Foster Hewitt because of Chuck's running commentary of the play, and later, Coach, as he realized the boy had a solid grasp of the game.

Chuck had never felt the thrill of the cold air on his face as he broke in on the net and never felt the crunch of the boards or the unforgiving hardness of the ice. He had longed for the pleasure of tucking the puck into the far post and making the red light shine. In all his life, Chuck had never laced on a skate.

It was during these times together on the cold benches that Smith called him 'Coach Chuck'. The town had never come close to making the young man a coach, but let him open bench doors at Saturday morning minor hockey games. The close-minded local hockey elite could never admit that Chuck, the boy with the limp, would have been the best coach the town could ever see.

"Who's your duded up friend?" Smith spat into the dust and leaned on the weathered rack of his truck.

"Mike Donovan." Mike stepped forward. The old farmer reached down and took his hand. Donovan did not flinch at the mixture of grain dust and farm related unknowns on Smith's hand.

"Ain't you a dandy," Smith doffed his battered, dirty forage cap, once army green. At first Mike thought it was in greeting, but Smith used it to mop his brow and jammed it askew, over his scraggly grey hair. "Damned bags are heavy."

Donovan walked around the truck, admiring the fact that it was still roadworthy. Or maybe not. Like Smith, it had seen better days.

"Looks like this thing could have been delivering barley to make booze for Al Capone," Mike laughed.

Smith paused. At his age, he rested between each bag. He laughed along with Mike. "Maybe," he said with a wink. "That distillery down in Windsor was always hungry. Now this stuff just feeds my sheep."

Donovan briefly pondered the fine line between the law and what put a few extra bucks into people's pockets. His view was that assault and murder were the big crimes, but the courts seemed to think property crime was more important. The worst sinners seemed to steal from the tax man or the rich. Mike's Irish background gave him a firm dislike for both groups. Avoiding the excise taxes did not seem a big deal to him, even though he had sworn to apply the law in every case.

He walked past the cab. The sudden vicious growl and barking of a big black dog startled him. The beast lunged at the partly open window, blowing slobber across the glass. Donovan jumped back. He then pressed his face close to the window.

"Get back, lie down!" He shouted. The dog whimpered and sat back, glaring, still resisting the domination.

"Don't mind Bucky," Smith said. "He just thinks he's God, and the world is his. Sleeps with me, though."

"It's okay," Donovan glanced across the street. "He reminds me of a hundred sled dogs, mean critters, that I saw up north."

"Sled dogs," Smith pondered. "I'd be lucky to get Bucky to move a foot from the wood stove in winter."

On the far side, on the spur beside the factory, several boxcars waited for a load. Just up the way, another stood out. Mike realized he saw what Blatchford had probably seen, 315387, alone up the hump line, waiting for its next mysterious journey.

"Do you come here often? Ever see anything strange over there?" Mike nodded at the factory.

"Well, I come here a bit. You never know about when Clem's going to decide to run this mechanical clap trap, so I bring grain down to wait in line. Clem says it's going to rain soon and he'll have more water. I think he's crazy, listens to that Gordon Gee government guy on the radio. The Almanac says dry to October. I'll go with them, but Clem's the guy who decides, so..."

"What about over there?" Donovan was tolerant, but wanted to end Smith's meandering.

The old farmer looked across to the rail cars, scratching his head. He had forgotten the second part of Donovan's question.

"You're the second stranger that's been here in the past bit. A young guy with that cute daughter of Millie's. If there ever was a gal making me wish I was fifty years younger, that's her." He smiled and gazed down the road to town, raising a frown from Chuck and making Mike frustrated.

"Over there," he nodded again.

"Well, that young guy, now I was resting inside in the shade, so got to watch it all. He wandered over the road and started fooling with that old boxcar up the way. Next thing I know, that jerk Winslow comes out. I can see he was mad, stalking stiff legged up to the young'un. They was on the far side so all I could see was feet under the car, and I couldn't hear nothing. Anyway, the young guy comes back around the car and looking back at Winslow, like he was upset. Maybe Winslow said something bad. He's like that, a bit of a jerk, and he couldn't play hockey." Smith rested on a bag of barley and appeared to be setting in for a long story. Winslow's lack of hockey playing ability seemed to seal the man's character in Smith's mind.

"So the guy comes back. He and that Kat take a blanket and head over the tailrace to the river. They was up for some fun, I thought." Smith winked at Donovan. Chuck stared at the ground. "I finished up and pull out towards home." He nodded up the road, away from town.

"Anyway, damned Bucky throws up on the seat, so I just get up there past the trees and pull over to clean it up, nothing worse than the smell of dog puke in the heat. I was kind of out of sight, but I could see back through the trees. Winslow come out and crossed the road. He took the way over to the intake catwalk. Maybe he thought Clem was inside, but he must have figured he was out of sight. He took a revolver out of his pocket, one of those little snub-nosed women's things." Smith sounded disdainful, as if the gun was another reflection on Winslow's manhood.

"He looked at it and then crept into the woods towards where the two snuck off. I got done with Bucky's mess and went home. Didn't want no part of a gunfight. I wasn't worried. Winslow doesn't have any guts, anyway."

Donovan made some notes. He headed across the road, leaving Chuck and Smith arguing over some long ago hockey game.

Mike's experience at the phantom boxcar almost duplicated Blatchford's, except, when he flashed his railway cop badge at Winslow, the little man backed off and became nervous.

"What's the story of this car? Do you use it?"

"About once a month, when we get an extra shipment, it's reserved for a special Toronto customer." Winslow was quick on his feet.

"Who owns it?"

"I guess the CSR, maybe the customer."

Winslow was nervous. Obviously, the cop suspected. Blatchford's snooping had been bad enough. This cop was serious trouble. The shipper did not like it when Donovan made notes. He wished he could see what Mike wrote.

"I'm investigating the terrible accident we had up in Goderich." Mike wanted the man to think no one was considering foul play. "Did you know Bill Blatchford?"

"Never heard of him."

"Did you talk with a young guy about this car a few weeks ago?"

"No," Winslow lied. Mike made a note.

"Do you know Al O'Connell?"

"The railway engineer, yes, I saw him at Millie's beer parlour a few times."

"At the beer parlour?"

"I was handing out Temperance Society cards," Winslow answered hurriedly, as if Mike had caught him visiting the slippery slope to Hell. "I was trying to get the alcoholic sinners to repent."

"Is that the only time you ever saw him?"

"Yes,"

Another lie, Donovan noted in his book.

"Where were you the night of the accident?" Mike consulted his notes and gave the date.

"I was home for supper, then I came here to finish up some paper-work." His lip and jaw had stopped hurting, but Winslow instinctively rubbed where O'Connell had hit him.

No alibi... motive? Donovan wrote, adding, *careless dresser*, as if that was a blot on Winslow's character, like the ink stain beneath his shirt pocket that had defeated attempts to wash it out. Mike straightened his tie, offsetting Winslow's sloppy appearance.

"I might want to talk to you again."

Chuck and Smith were now well into the season of 1952, enjoying some laughs.

"No," Chuck was adamant, "Jackson scored those three goals the season before, the one time we beat Clinton."

Smith and Coach Chuck both agreed that Clinton was lower than the low. Maitland had only ever defeated the Clinton team one time in all the years they competed. The pair quickly jumped two seasons to Maitland's next victory over the luckless Lucknow Millers.

Donovan wandered over the tailrace bridge and found a stump in the shade of a willow. He relaxed at the sound of water trickling over the weir and birds chattering in the gentle breeze. It reminded him of the times he would be out on the land, hunting with his Cree friend, Billy Pyne. This was the world he wished he lived in.

Chapter Ten

Donovan's offer to buy lunch enticed Chuck to drive to Goderich. "It was frustrating talking to Mr. Smith." Chuck made it a question. He knew and loved the fact the farmer hockey fan loved to tell long stories with plenty of detours. Chuck knew the names of Smith's ewes, rams, cows, roosters and dogs, and the unending litany of humour and mayhem that each created. He also knew that his friend's stories eased the loneliness and family history that had led to Smith's struggling along in a farmer's version of retirement. It could be less enjoyable for strangers.

"It was inefficient, let's say," Donovan chuckled, hanging on as Chuck dove into a sharp, blind curve on the county road and came back to their side of the road just in front of a farm tractor coming the other way. The farmer shook his fist. Chuck honked the horn.

"That's Blankhurst," Chuck laughed. "He drives around on the tractor just to get away from his wife. We sometimes meet at the Supertest and he buys me a Coke. I taught his son how to do a slap-shot on the concrete pad out behind their barn. The kid's playing semi-pro somewhere now."

"Smith wasn't too bad," Mike returned to Chuck's question as his heart-rate returned to normal. "I once took three days to complete an interview with an Indian elder up north. It was about a murder and a hard story. We did the smoking thing and everything, not the tobacco ceremony, just smoking. We both smoked pipes. It cost me a whole pouch of Amphora, and all the while he was complaining because he liked the red pouch and I smoke brown. I think he dragged the story out just to get more tobacco."

Mike left Chuck sitting in the shade sucking on a Coke and went into the police office.

"Did you get any prints?"

"One set, a thumb and partial fingers on the wrench, nothing on the wood. There are no matches on file so far, but checking takes time. I wish there was an automatic way to do it."

"Maybe one day they'll have a fancy gizmo for it," Donovan said.

"All I can say is Blatchford's prints weren't on it. We got the autopsy report, and they copied his prints. There was no blood on Blatchford's boots. Here are the pictures of the tread."

"I'd like a copy of the report," the progress pleased Mike. "Did they say how he died? Were there any bullet holes or stab wounds?"

"No bullets. He was pretty banged up to sort out if it was stabbing. A heavy blow to the head, they think he hit his head about three times. It could have been from the accident, but it's unlikely. All three blows were near the same spot on his left temple. The coroner says they bled pretty good. I guess you were right. It's murder. No one could kill themselves that way."

"That just tells us the killer was probably right-handed if he was facing Blatchford. Not much help. I've only seen righties around here."

"The lefties all left town," Bowers deadpanned. "Someone was hoping the crash would be worse than it was. Maybe it would have if the empty coach hadn't been there to absorb some of the energy. The longhood forward helped protect the cab as well. The wrench is the odd ball clue. What was it doing in the cab? Someone took it there on purpose because they planned to kill with it, first degree murder. It's a hanging offence."

"Jones," Bowers said, "maybe he used it to defeat the dead-man switch. They all do it."

"So either it had nothing to do with anything or it was used to kill him. If the last, then Jones did it, if his prints are on it."

"We need Jones' prints."

"I have his prints," Bowers said. "We wanted to make sure who he was. When we found him, he was just a blubbering mess."

The two men closely compared Jones' prints to the photograph of the lifted prints in the OPP report. They did not match.

"Gloves?" Bowers asked.

"Could be," Donovan thought it logical. Railway men always wore gloves. "I wish we could tell whose prints those are."

"I want to talk with Jones again."

"Too late. He left town, went back to Guelph."

"I'll get to him there. He sure recovered quick."

"Jones didn't do it," Bowers suggested.

"I'm not convinced," Donovan frowned. "He's still the prime suspect, but he had to have an accomplice to set the signal. Jones was the only one we know was there unless..." He gazed off into space.

"Unless what?"

"He was supposed to die, too. I still don't see his motive. Store all the evidence safely."

Chuck pulled into the White Rose service station. Donovan paid the smiling attendant a dollar for the gasoline. Webster would scream blue-murder at the expense.

"Thanks, Mr. Donovan," Chuck said. "That'll last me a week."

"By the way," Chuck reached under the seat and extracted a comic book with a garish cover depicting a square-jawed cop socking a thug in the jaw. "I thought your name was familiar. Is this you?" He showed Mike the magazine.

Special Agent, Mike Donovan.

"Didn't I read about you in this comic book?" Bisco chuckled.

"It must have been my uncle. He went to the States." Mike examined the comic book.

"That couldn't be me, see? This guy's a lefty. I'm right handed, and never hit someone in the face. You'll break your hand. Besides, in the

RCMP they trained us to be polite. 'Excuse me, mister violent murderer you, please come along so we can hang you?'"

"The Forest Ranger in a funny hat," Chuck eased the Olds into Victoria Street and squealed the tires a few yards down the blacktop.

"I might need you more," Mike smiled. "How would you like to drive to Guelph sometime, if you have any tires left?"

"Oh, that'd be great. Could Kat come?"

Donovan wanted to visit Blatchford's widow and track down Jones.

"I don't think that would be a good idea this time."

***

Chuck parked the Olds on the far side of the street opposite a small, nicely painted bungalow. It was a fine example of 'war housing' with a white picket fence and a scruffy yard of mowed grass, languishing in the dry summer heat. Donovan got out and headed towards the gate. He had a small package of Blatchford's belongings from the locomotive cab and his locker in the Goderich bunkhouse. The notebook was not in the package. It was evidence.

No car in the drive. Maybe she's out.

Mike knew Blatchford owned a Plymouth. The door opening to his second knock surprised Donovan.

"I'm Michael Donovan." Mike flashed his railway badge. He always omitted his title, Constable. People seemed to clam up when he said it.

"Irene Blatchford, how can I help you, Constable?"

"Mike will do," Donovan smiled. "I'm sorry to bother you when you're grieving, but I'm investigating Bill's death. I'm sorry for your loss."

"Come in." Irene Blatchford wore a fluffy pink housecoat. She could have been naked underneath. Her combed out hair and her face softened with makeup. Bright red lipstick highlighted her lips. She smelled of rose scented soap and peach shampoo.

She doesn't look like a grieving widow.

Donovan doffed his fedora and stepped inside.

Irene escorted Mike to the kitchen with its chromed table set and metal edged counters covered in mottled green vinyl. A modern electric percolator had just finished bubbling.

"Coffee?"

Mike accepted. He placed his hat and notebook on the table and put the package at one end.

"Did Bill have any enemies?" Donovan sipped a perfectly made cup of A and P Bokar coffee, the strong kind that came in the black bag.

"Did someone kill him?" Irene did not seem surprised.

"That's what I'm trying to find out. There are a lot of questions about the crash. Bill was too good an engineer to have made all the mistakes needed to wreck the engine." Donovan thought praising her dead husband might put Mrs. Blatchford more at ease.

"He was full of himself. Maybe he was thinking of one of his floozies."

"What do you mean, Mrs. Blatchford?"

"You can call me Irene," she smiled. "Bill had a bunch of women he was screwing regularly or as one-night stands. Maybe a jealous husband got him, or he was daydreaming."

"You don't seem upset." Mike sipped his coffee. Taking notes seemed to be inappropriate.

"I pretended I was stupid. He paid the bills and there were railway benefits. All I had to do was keep house for him and jump into the sack. It wasn't bad at all. I get some insurance, but now I have to work in the station diner where I met Bill. I guess it'll be back there for me."

"The funeral will be expensive. The railway is complaining about paying for an accident that was Bill's fault. If someone killed him, they might pay quicker. I hope you don't find out he killed himself. There would be no insurance then."

"I'm absolutely certain he didn't kill himself." Mike thought Irene would get along with his boss, Webster. They both seemed to enjoy counting money.

"Do you have the names of these lovers?" This suggestion of several new suspects daunted Donovan. The problem with secret lovers was they were secret. No doubt, Blatchford's harem would spread everywhere.

"Some little floozy up at Maitland was the last I heard about. He was too smart to touch any railway women. He wanted promotion too bad to get some husband, or a jilted woman bad-mouthing him to the railway. I don't have any names. They live in town here and up the line. He had a Toronto run on the spare board before the Goderich job came up. There are probably some there."

Irene reached over the table and took Donovan's hand.

"I know I sound awful, Mike. Bill was just a meal ticket. I'm not that kind of woman." Her face softened, and she leaned forward so her high-lighted eyes peeked up at Mike. "I loved him. When we got married, it all changed. I'll love again." She squeezed his hand.

Oh, my! Mike gently withdrew his hand. *She is attractive, Kat and her. Blatchford liked good looks.*

Mike finished his coffee. A victim's wife trying to seduce the cop and being the actual killer was a movie cliché. He had seen that Bogart movie, too. Donovan was no Bogart, this was no movie, and Irene was so far down the list of suspects, it seemed unlikely.

She could have had someone else do it. If Blatchford's running around on her was a motive, she was good at hiding her anger. Bill was her meal ticket. Mike doubted she would change that deliberately, unless a better offer came along.

Irene looked in the package of Bill's belongings.

"Weren't there any sun glasses? Bill had a nice pair of aviation glasses he got from some pilot friend during the war. He always carried them."

"I cleaned out the wrecked cab and his locker myself," Mike said. "I didn't see any glasses, or even broken ones. The engine was in terrible shape. Everything from his body is in the package."

"I'll let you know if I learn anything. That coffee was excellent. It deserves a second, sometime." Mike flirted back.

Irene took his arm and led him to the door.

"I hope you solve it soon," she squeezed his arm. "Come for a second cup, anytime."

As she reached for the doorknob, the door swung open. George Jones' eyes were full of surprise, bewilderment and fear.

"Hello George," Mike smiled. "I didn't expect to see you here."

"I'm just coming to give Irene my condolences and a few things to help." He held a large paper bag of groceries and a plain brown one from the liquor store.

"I'm just leaving," said Mike. "I would like to talk with you again sometime soon. How's the head?"

Mike smiled at Jones, tipped his hat towards the blushing Irene, and placed it on his head. The door closed behind him as he descended the steps. He faintly heard what seemed to be Irene saying, *Shh*, and giggling. He would not need to interview Jones just yet. The man had just told Donovan most of what he needed to know.

Motive! Donovan made a note *for two... and an accomplice.*

A dark blue '54 Plymouth sat in the driveway. Irene had climbed a few spaces up Donovan's suspect list. George Jones solidified his position as suspect number one. The motive was big, but the method he used seemed wrong. It would have made more sense to throw Blatchford's body into the river as they crossed the bridge and then claim it was suicide. The motive would still be there, but there would be no proof.

If he did it, someone else had to set the semaphore at Meneset. Was the person Harold saw limping up the hill, Irene? Why did Jones end up battered against a tree? Maybe he and Blatchford fought and Jones got hurt badly before he killed Bill... Too many questions, too many answers and nothing fit.

"It's a busy place," Chuck said as Mike slid into the front seat.

"I think it's a routine here." Donovan muttered, staring at the Plymouth. Pieces had fallen into place. Jones was the first name to be on all the lists. Donovan hated the obvious.

Did Albert O'Connell know how to run an RS3? He and Jones were still neck and neck.

Were Jones and Irene working together, or did he act on his own? He looked at Bisco as the lad concentrated on the unfamiliar streets.

Even Chuck's still on some of my lists, especially the motive. Damn it, everyone involved seems to share the top of the motive list.

"Swing by the railway yard. I have to do some research."

Chuck happily cooled his heels at the lunch counter in the passenger terminal as Mike explored personnel files in the main office. He discovered Jones' spare board status. His off days certainly gave him plenty of time to be with Irene Blatchford while Bill was safely on the rails. It seemed a cozy arrangement with no strings. Why would Jones want to change it? Mike remembered Jones in the hospital saying Blatchford did not care for his wife and disrespected her. Maybe Jones actually loved Irene. *More motive!*

Mike also discovered O'Connell had once applied for diesel training. He had passed the tests, including a practical in an RS1, but they rejected Al because of his looming retirement. There was a handwritten note in his file, "*Made threats when rejected*".

Mike made notes.

"I'll have the liver with fries and large milk," Donovan sat beside Chuck at the counter. Bisco sipped on a coffee, scraping up the remnants of coconut-cream pie in front of him. Mike added a slice of pie to his order.

"You're an expensive date," Donovan stared at the bill as the cashier merrily rang up the total. Chuck had downed a club sandwich, fries and his own milk. "Four bucks!"

"Think of me as the son you never had," Bisco laughed.

Chuck had accidentally hit a nerve in Mike. The major regret in Donovan's life was not having a family. Once his mom had passed, he was on his own. He had no brothers or sisters. His Grandmother had constantly admonished his mother about having an only child.

What kind of good Catholic family is that?

It had been a source of tension between the women, the one big dark spot in Mike's childhood. He loved them both. Being an only child had left him self-centred until fate as the RCMP had plunked him down in the black spruce, surrounded by natives. The Cree had taught him humility.

Donovan added three dollars' worth of gas from the Supertest in Maitland to the total of Chuck's expenses. Donovan smiled. Webster would have lots to whine about when the job was done. The owner of the gas station, in his grease stained coveralls, happily filled the tank. Chuck usually took only a gallon or fifty cents worth at most.

Donovan was happy O'Connell's second place on his suspect list had strengthened and pushed Chuck into a more remote fourth, now behind Irene Blatchford's potential collusion with Jones.

If Mike could tie that boxcar into the death, not to mention those nameless lovers, he would have a few more suspects. *Damn!*

They headed to Millie's.

16

Chapter Eleven

Millie was busy with no time to flirt. She took the time to set a coffee in front of Donovan at her personal table and went off to talk with an officious-looking stranger at a table near the office. The man was chain-smoking Export A's. From time to time, she disappeared to retrieve some papers. Mike pulled out his notebook. He stuffed his pipe and drew hard on the lighter, raising an aromatic cloud.

He had uncovered a lot of new information and needed to sort it out. Motives had appeared everywhere, especially for Jones. Either Jones did it with Irene's help, or someone drove to Meneset, set the signals to stop, unhitched the train, clobbered Jones, killed Blatchford and sent the engine on its death trip. They then drove away, possibly back to Maitland Station… premeditated and well planned. Whoever did it had detailed knowledge of how railways work.

But if it was someone else, why wasn't Jones left in the cab dead, like Blatchford?

He created a new list of those who knew what the semaphore meant and how to set it. Jones would have needed an accomplice to set the signal. He could have coached Irene Blatchford. Other than that, it meant only operating train crew, and perhaps Chuck. He added Ed, who fit on every list but opportunity and motive, as did Bobby Ellis and Walter Edwards. Perhaps the person Harold saw had nothing to do with the murder. He could only fit the "jerk" Winslow into two lists, motive and opportunity. Mike wondered if Winslow had any railway experience beyond stuffing boxcars.

I need to get a few more off the suspect list, he thought.

Millie finally seemed to be done with her guest. The man stayed at the far table but seemed content that Millie had provided enough records. She brought two coffees and sat opposite Mike.

"No wine today?" Mike teased.

"Shh," Millie looked a little worried. "Technically, the dining room can only sell booze with food. He's from the Liquor Control Board, trying to find out if I'm bootlegging. Not me. I'm not greedy, but he likes to push people around. He would love to catch me serving booze in here."

"But maybe my big, strong cop friend can protect me." Millie smiled and winked. Different attractive women had never hit on Donovan twice in one day. It felt good. And Millie was mature and sensible.

"I have little authority with those guys, but if I knew you better, I'd be a character witness." He sounded serious.

"You could get to know a lot more about me," she winked again.

Donovan sighed and tried to ask a safe question. It would not be the first time he stuck his size ten shoes in his mouth.

"How did you and Al get together?"

The scowl on Millie's face made him regret it immediately.

"Oh, I'm sorry." His face matched his hair.

Millie sat quietly, her face softened. She seemed to have reached a decision.

"I guess I asked for that." She wasn't flirting any longer. "Somehow, I want to be honest with you. I want you to like me, so you need to see all the warts before you decide."

"I like you already," Donovan's face had returned to normal. His freckles hardly showed. "You don't need to tell me anything. That's none of my business."

"I would like it all to be your business."

Is she flirting again? Mike wondered, feeling a dry spruce twig under his shoe.

"Go ahead," he smiled.

"You're a smart man. I know you already did the arithmetic and fig-ured Kathleen was born in '39 or early '40. It doesn't seem to jibe with what I said about my husband."

"You caught me," admitted Mike.

"My husband, Freddy and I were sweethearts in high school. I was an excellent student and got my Grade Twelve. My Dad wouldn't think of a girl wasting her life taking Grade Thirteen and maybe university. I graduated and took a job with the CSR. Things were busier here and there was a lunch-counter down at the station back then."

Millie paused and frowned at the liquor inspector. He was smiling. That made her nervous. Maybe the numbers exposed the case of beer she would take upstairs to Al's room. She had fudged the sales in the bar, but maybe she had slipped up.

"Freddy was lovely, but not school material. He quit and joined the navy. They weren't taking many men then. The war seemed unlikely, but his family knew the Member of Parliament, some friend of Macken-zie-King, and he got him in. He was gone a long time." Millie seemed ready to cry at the memory despite the decades since.

"I was lonely, and I guess gullible. Al was a regular at the lunch-counter. There were a lot of trains a day back then. Al ran the yard switcher. He seemed mature and romantic, well travelled compared to Freddy. It's hard to believe he was handsome, too. One thing led to an-other, and he got me pregnant. Then he dumped me. He said he didn't need a kid in his life." Millie dabbed her eyes. "It turned out he was mar-ried already, just not living at home."

"So that's why you were so mad at Blatchford? It was a rerun."

Millie nodded. "I was desperate, but before I showed, Freddie came back on leave. That was in August '39. I talked him into marrying me. He was a pushover. At least my baby would have a father. He was my genuine love. We talked about buying a hotel once he left the navy. His leave ended the day they declared war. I never saw him again. He was on a Corvette that went down in the middle of the Atlantic."

"I got a job at the Goderich training base. I wouldn't have to see Al every day, at least. Kathleen was born in early '40, and I just carried on."

"How did Al worm his way back in?" Mike saw Millie as a sister, at least.

"The war depleted the local male population my age by about a dozen. The men who were eligible didn't want a widow with a kid. I got lonely and came back to the railway. Al got what he wanted, and I could at least pretend I was worth something. He never acknowledged Kathleen until he found out about Blatchford having sex with her. For him, it was just another reason to hate Blatchford. Kat still isn't important. Al won't be welcome much longer."

"The part about the hotel was mostly how it happened, except the old guy selling lowered the price and gave me a mortgage for sex." Millie did not seem embarrassed. Donovan could not see her face. She hoped Mike would not hate her for it. What Millie had done did not differ from Irene Blatchford's story.

"Fortunately, the old man had a heart attack one night soon after we signed the papers. It was horrible. I snuck out and let someone else find him."

Mike frowned.

"Oh, I was certain he was dead or I would have called for help. I wouldn't let a dog die if I could save it, let alone a generous, lonely old man."

"Life's rules don't always seem like rules," Mike said.

"The family put up a fuss, but the documents were all legal, signed by lawyers and everything, so I just paid into the estate. Things stayed busy until after the Korean War and then slid. I had paid it all off by then. It's the only reason I'm still in business, that and drunken farm boys at least," Millie laughed.

The inspector called her over, still smiling, and before long, Millie smiled too. They had a coffee, and the man left. Millie went into the kitchen to prepare the evening menu. Donovan sat.

No one's life is simple, he thought.

"I have to go down to the station," Donovan shouted to Millie through the kitchen door. "See you later."

Mike did not know why he thought he had to tell Millie where he had gone.

Chuck was in the station, sipping a free coffee and reading the Toronto Star Weekly. He giggled over some comic strip.

"Got a minute?" Mike sat beside him. "I have some questions. I want to scratch you off my list of suspects."

"I'm a suspect?" Chuck was excited. "Wow, that's great. You're the first one to think I might have done something big."

"If you did it," Donovan tried to look serious, "you'll have a stretched neck to go with that swelled head."

"Can I buy you off?" Chuck handed Mike a mug of fresh hot coffee.

Donovan lit his pipe, just as Train 110, fronted by the Pacific, passed the station at yard speed and headed towards Goderich.

"He's early," Mike said to Ed.

"CSR found an RS1 to handle 100 and 101. Al is back on his old duties. They have to run the grain down to the dock. They'll be doing that all the time. The RS1 is about shot and they don't want it overworked. It'll just handle the consist." Ed resumed reading the sports pages of the London newspaper.

"Chuck, tell me all about what you learned when riding with Ed in the RS1."

"Damned little," Ed growled. He listened while pretending to read the paper.

"It was long ago. I was just a kid. I learned the controls, and how to couple and do switches, but I was too little to actually do it."

"Did he ever teach you the signals, like the semaphore and the lights?"

"No, I remember he told me I'd have to get more schooling first."

"So you don't know what they mean or how they work?"

"Nope, I can't figure out why a train can roar past a signal when only the top one is green and the bottom two are red."

"Complicated," Donovan agreed. "Have you ever been to Meneset Station?"

"Just rode through on the train. I never got off and have never been there otherwise. Am I off the hook?"

"Ninety-nine percent." Mike closed his notebook.

Chuck returned to his comics. Donovan sucked on his pipe and thought. He had taken Chuck totally off the list, down with Millie and Kathleen.

A place Chuck would love to be, Mike thought.

He looked at Bisco through a blue haze of Amphora smoke. He had seen less likely romances become flourishing marriages.

Donovan thought about the wrench, the key to the whole murder. He briefly wondered where Blatchford's sunglasses went.

Boxcar 315387 was still a big loose end, and might yet hold the answer to fingering the murderer. What had Blatchford written about it? Donovan reviewed the battered notebook in his mind. It seems to be always the last week of the month at Mile 47.

Next week, Donovan consulted the railway calendar on the wall, the one with the spectacular pictures of the Rockies. Donovan wondered if it disappointed some foreign tourists going from Windsor to Toronto that flat Elgin County did not look like the mountains in the posters.

Monday morning, I have to see what's happening.

He stepped out to the platform and looked over the yard towards the engine shed. A plan came together. He would give up his idea of returning to Guelph for the weekend. Donovan would have to be up early on Monday morning.

He smoothed his jacket sleeves, straightened his tie, and headed for Millie's hotel. Bowers worked Saturdays. Maybe he had more on the wrench, and he needed to be told of Jones' motive.

Al and the crew would spend the weekend at home in Guelph, taking a special manifest train, 211 eastbound Friday and returning late Sunday with whatever freight had accumulated on the weekend, fronting another special grain manifest called train 210. Harvest season made a good profit.

It was Mike's turn to buy Millie a bottle of wine.

***

Chuck's Olds jerked to a top in front of the Goderich police station. The town was busy on Saturday mornings. Donovan climbed from the back seat and smiled at Chuck and Kat. Hr had invited Kat on this ride. Mike played cupid and insisted she ride with Chuck.

Who knows? He thought.

Mike rubbed his head. A bottle of wine was a bad thing when it turned into two.

"I told you so. Blatchford found out and tried to kill Jones. Then he killed himself." Bowers seemed sure.

"Or Irene Blatchford set the signal and Jones killed Blatchford and knocked himself out, jumping off the train. Or they had a fight and Jones got beat up before killing Blatchford." Mike was still doubtful.

"Oh, I have an addition to the OPP report on the wrench. They delayed it because the sample was so small. The lab thinks there are two types of blood on the wrench, type O, same as Blatchford's type. The other was AB, very rare."

"Great, so the wrench could have hit eighty percent of us on the head."

"Jones blood is AB. I sweet-talked Rita at the hospital. They gave him a unit. They keep any donor with a special type on standby. Funny enough, in this case, it was a CNR brakeman."

"Looks like both Blatchford's and Jones' heads had a meeting with the wrench." Donovan deadpanned. "That seems to juggle my suspects list a bit. Jones is weaker, but could still have done it. A desirable woman is motive enough."

"Linking Irene Blatchford and Jones makes it interesting. It sounds like a movie."

"She even tried to come on to me," Mike smiled. "She's pretty. Just call me Bogy."

"No wonder," Bowers said. "A single, good looking middle-aged man with a job, all these desperate middle-aged women would want you, especially one who just lost her meal ticket."

"Desperate, eh, thanks a lot, and she has a back-up meal ticket. Jones actually seems to be nicer than the opinion I have of Blatchford. Run me over to Meneset. I want to see where you found Jones."

"Chuck," Mike leaned on the Olds as Bowers went to retrieve the cruiser. "I'm going over to Meneset station. I'll need some time, but can you come pick me up on your way home? Here's a buck for the soda fountain."

"No thanks, Mike," Bisco frowned, "I'll pay for Kat. See you at Meneset."

Donovan and Bowers headed around the square, leaving town. Chuck escorted Kat to the drugstore, arm in arm in the pleasant sunshine.

"There's where we found Jones."

Bowers pointed to a large oak tree about ten yards down the steep river bank opposite the station. From their spot on the tracks, they could see the disturbance left by the rescue squad.

"Jones must have fallen down there with the train stopped," Donovan said, checking the angle to the station door. "I don't think he did it. The blood on the wrench seems to say someone clobbered him too, and he couldn't have set up the train after being hit."

"Damn, Donovan, I originally wanted a nice simple accident, then ordinary suicide. You're making it too much fun for me now. This is the most interesting thing that has happened in my entire career. How did you learn to work like this?"

"I once had a case, way up north. This Cree man died. It looked like he was chopping down a tree and it fell on him. It didn't look right to me, the wrong angle for the tree and all that. Anyway, I checked into it and discovered that he a neighbour had killed him. The guy hit him with the back side of an axe, then felled a tree right on top of him. It almost looked real. My clue was that a branch punctured the dead man, but the wound didn't bleed like it should have. He was already dead when the tree hit him."

"The dead guy had been messing with the killer's twelve-year-old daughter. That was the motive. The father broke down, crying in my office and confessed everything, including how the victim had raped the girl. In the old days, the community would have met and handled the rape. Who knows what their decision would be, healing, expulsion or the guy would have ended up dead, anyway?"

"In Canada, I would have investigated the rape, sent a report recommending charges and waited. It was a serious crime. If a Crown Attorney in Edmonton wanted publicity, they might have charged the guy, flown him south and almost certainly convicted him. More likely, they would ignore it as a native problem and unimportant. We saw that a lot. I let the death remain an accident."

"I guess there's justice and there's justice," Bowers said. "I won't feel so guilty when I let some kid off for being a kid and just scare them good. It works most times. Did you ever arrest anyone?"

"I had the lowest arrest record in the north," Donovan bragged. "My Corporal at Fort Chip didn't like it. He must have gotten a bonus for numbers."

"I have a hunch." Mike walked along the tracks towards Goderich. He examined both sides of the ballast. About two engine lengths along, he stopped and stared at the river side ties and gravel. There were some deep impressions that the boots of someone landing hard could have caused. Past that, he saw some other disturbed stones.

"If the train were speeding up, and the killer jumped here, they might have lost their balance and did a header into the gravel." Donovan's Brownie camera came out, and he snapped some shots. "I think we have just eliminated Jones."

"Could be," Bowers agreed. "That leaves O'Connell as the likely killer."

"It seems obvious," Mike agreed.

Al's obvious guilt was the problem. The only time the obvious killer was guilty was when the police arrived and found a husband or wife standing over their spouse's body. Like that Clinton kid in the Goderich jail whom everyone had already convicted on circumstantial evidence, even though the trial was weeks away. It was too obvious for Mike, but the OPP had that problem.

"Let's look at the station."

"No one works at the station anymore. The conductor sells tickets if anyone gets on board." Mike examined the locks on the semaphore levers and the call box. He felt along the rafter plate above the box and retrieved a worn brass key. It opened all the padlocks.

"How did you know that was there?"

"Railway people are predictable. Crew are supposed to carry the keys, but sometimes they forget or lose them. Most crew would hide a key here somewhere. Now you know too."

"Damn!" exclaimed Bowers.

"Yes," Mike agreed, "but it narrows it down to a railway-man setting the signals to stop."

"Where are those kids?" The two men leaned on the cruiser in the Meneset parking lot up the hill from the station. Donovan sucked on his pipe. Bowers lit his third duMaurier. The Olds appeared and skidded to a stop beside the men.

"Good thing this is OPP jurisdiction out here, lad. Driving like that should cost you at least ten bucks."

Bowers tried to frown at Chuck. The boy ignored him. The Chief left in the cruiser, throwing up his own bit of gravel.

Donovan watched Bowers' car disappear. He looked at Bowers' skid marks in the small gravel covered parking lot. The only skid marks were Chuck's and the Chief's. It had not rained since the murder. Every local driver, with any experience, seemed to throw gravel whenever they pulled in or out.

If the murderer drove a car here, then they did not spin their tires. A nervous killer would likely have spun tires in their desire to get away. Why not? A hardened killer or an inexperienced driver, or a woman, he wondered.

"Sorry we're late." Chuck grinned at Donovan.

"You guys having too much fun?" Donovan asked.

"No," Chuck blushed, looking at Kat, who stared at the ground. "Someone stole the sign for the station. I couldn't find the turn. We ended up at the airport terminal. There was a neat little airplane there, and we kind of checked it out." Again, he looked at Kat and blushed. "Anyway, here we are."

"I've never been here before," said Kat. "Just went by on the train."

Mike got in the back seat and made a note. Gravel flew as they left the parking lot. Chuck did not know it, but he had permanently bumped himself onto the same list as Kat and Millie... the innocent list. He no longer needed Bob Hope for an alibi.

17

Chapter Twelve

Mike Donovan slipped out of the doorway from his room. The worn hallway carpet muffled his leather shoes. The creaking of the steps defeated his attempt at stealth. He needed to be in place in the railway yard before O'Connell and his crew appeared for their day's work. Mike would have loved a coffee but did not want to risk Millie knowing he was up and about. She was already in the kitchen getting ready for breakfast. There were regular customers, and Al always wanted coffee with toast and a packed lunch. Mike did not want Millie accidentally letting Al know the cop was on the loose. He slipped out the front door, easing it shut. The latch clicked, and he hurried down the half-lit street.

Across the dining room, Millie smiled from the kitchen doorway. Somehow, a cop sneaking around, especially if it was Mike Donovan, reassured her.

The night man was busy keeping steam up in the Pacific. He had rolled the engine out of the shed. Donovan kept the station between them as he crossed the parking lot, detouring around Ed's Buick and picking his way over the main and lead tracks. He passed behind a boxcar that screened him from the engine. The caboose crew would soon wake up with Walter and Bobby in the bunkhouse on the far side of the yard. Mike was sure he was unseen.

It was hard navigating in the gloom of the engine shed. Mike stumbled against discarded equipment and boxes before finding a place at a dirt smudged window. He sacrificed his clean handkerchief to make a peephole. The engine man had a bench and chair on the far side where he ate his midnight lunch and played solitaire while waiting for the Pacific to cool down. The place had once been busy, with three track bays occupied with engines and a strong arm turntable to sort them out. Now there was only the Pacific in action. The middle track hosted an old steam engine, a 2-6-0 that hadn't seen service in years.

Donovan wore blue coveralls for his adventure. The camera and note book fit easily into the loose pockets. He ducked below the bench to light his pipe and then settled in on a wooden barrel of track spikes, waiting for action.

The eastern horizon showed at the pre-dawn. The engine crew appeared, and the night man had a brief chat with O'Connell and retrieved his lunch bucket from the far bay. He sniffed the faint aroma of Amphora, but Donovan was out of sight behind the old Mogul. Without spotting Donovan, the night-man went home. Mike watched.

The Pacific made up its train and then waited on the lead, with the tail and caboose well down the mill spur. The morning consist from Goderich to Guelph passed, heading east at 8:30. Ten minutes later, train 111 eased onto the main line and steamed away. Boxcar 315387 had not appeared.

Now that it was light, Donovan could see the interior of the engine shed. In the unused bay, amongst the shelves of bearings, sleeves, links, and chains, there were two identical boxes of tools. One was dusty and had been there for years. One was fresh. The dusty container held a large, well-worn wrench. The newer one did not. Mike picked up the old wrench, covering his hand with coal soot and dust. It was identical to the murder weapon. Chuck had brought the newer box minus the wrench from Ed's office the day Mike bumped his leg on it. Donovan knew where the killer had found his weapon. It had been such a minor event, and he had not noted the detailed content of the box.

The box with the wrench must have been in Ed's office before the murder. Strange how these little things add up. Who had access? Unfortunately, just about everyone.

The Cree hunters had taught him patience. On Wednesday morning, the third day of watching, all paid off. As Mike looked, O'Connell backed the Pacific onto the spur and headed to the factory. He returned with several boxcars. 315387 trailed the bunch. Bobby was busy doing the coupling and switching as they juggled the lineup so that he hitched 315387 behind the engine tender. O'Connell drew the long line of boxcars and empty grain cars well down the line, preparing to back in for the caboose. Donovan took the opportunity, with the Pacific well away, to walk through the yard and into Ed's office.

"I need to catch 101 to Guelph," Mike said to Ed. Ed dropped the semaphore to stop the passenger train.

Mike ran over to the hotel.

"Millie, please ask Chuck to pick me up over on Highway 23 at the crossing below Listowel, about noon. I have to take a train ride there."

"Listowel, have you developed an interest in flax?"

"I always liked fine linen," Mike quipped. "There's something I need to look at."

Millie fussed over the kitchen counter as they talked.

"Here," she smiled, "I'd be sad if my favourite cop starved to death."

She handed Donovan a thick ham sandwich and a boiled egg, both wrapped in wax paper. "Here's some of my finest coffee." She winked.

"Is it Bokar?" asked Mike.

"Nope, my specialty is Chase... Chase and Sanborn. I like the Chase better." Millie winked.

Mike changed into his jacket and fedora and hurried to the station, stuffing the sandwich and thermos of coffee into his briefcase.

I might get to like the Chase too, thought Donovan. *It's a bit like that Cree children's game, where they all went into the bush and tried to catch one another without being caught. Once one did snag another, the pair would play the game together looking for more. What did they call it, Wolf and Rabbit?*

"I want off at Mile 47," Mike said to Harold.

Train 101 passed the crossing fifteen minutes ahead of O'Connell's manifest freight. Donovan hid out of sight in the trees past the cattle pens with a good view of the tracks.

Train 111 stopped short of the east switch to the siding. Bobby Ellis jumped off and hurried to uncouple the engine and 315387 from the train. They backed the boxcar into the siding with Bobby riding the fore-ladder. As Bobby uncoupled and set the brake on the boxcar, Donovan snapped a few pictures. In one photograph, Bobby was staring into the trees, straight at Donovan as if he had spotted the detective. Only Mike's training kept him from an instinctive duck. If he had moved, Bobby would likely have spotted him. Those Cree hunters had taught him to look for both shape and movement. It worked the other way if you were the prey.

The photos were clear enough, although sunglasses partly hid Bobby. He even had a shot of Edwards hanging out the fireman side window. O'Connell occupied the engineer's side, out of sight. As usual, Bobby rode the tender and reconnected the train. They disappeared to the east.

Donovan walked to the boxcar, trying to ignore the pungent smell of dried cattle droppings. He had an ear cocked for a truck, even though he did not think anyone would come before dark. Nothing was certain. Depressions made by the wheels of a large vehicle passed through the gate and up to the siding, directly where the boxcar sat. Broken dogwood stems suggested that the truck had been here in the past month. The crushed plants had only partly healed.

Billy Pyne taught me well, Donovan mused.

He carefully photographed the tracks and both sides of the boxcar.

The door had no lock. He slid it open with little effort. Furniture did not fill the car, but it made a substantial load, secured by straps. A hand written bill of lading lay on the floor at the door. Donovan removed his jacket and struggled into the car.

Another shirt ruined, he thought.

The load was worth thousands of dollars, although the only ones hurt were the tax man, unsuspecting partners in the factory, and the CSR, which missed freight charges they would not have received, anyway. He wondered how much the people buying the loot paid. There seemed to be a long list of accomplices, especially the CSR crew, who had to be paid off. He picked up the packing list.

Mike read through the paperwork, considering his options. The increasing heat as the morning sun beat down on the car stirred him to action. Donovan had a plan.

The easiest things to move were chairs. Mike extracted three from the load and dropped them onto the gravel. He tried to set the straps, so all looked normal. Once on the ground, Donovan hid the chairs in the bush. He rested on one while mopping the perspiration from his face. His armpits reminded him of Millie's love of cooking with garlic.

With any luck, whoever came for the load would be in a hurry and not read the packing-list. The buyer would discover the shortage when the loot arrived wherever it was going. They would blame the truck crew first, and afterwards perhaps Winslow, and others at the factory. Donovan had faith the crooks would fight amongst themselves, dealing out their own justice. It was not a good idea to steal from crooks. Thieves thinking someone had stolen from them usually lashed out.

Winslow might need his snub-nosed .38 after all. Donovan scowled. At least, if a gun was in play, it was best to know about it. He did not know where the gun might be. Likely, Winslow had bought a new one. Little guys loved the equalizer.

Highway 23 was a short walk along the side-road to Monkton. The track would have been quicker, but Mike wanted to come back by car to watch the shipment being unloaded. He found an overgrown lane through some maples where his car would be invisible from the road.

At the highway, Chuck had not arrived. Mike settled onto a deadfall at the edge of the roadside bush, hoping Chuck had received the message. He sipped coffee from the thermos and munched Millie's delicious sandwich. He enjoyed a second pipe-full and considered walking to the nearest phone when a car came from the south. It wasn't Chuck's Olds. Millie skidded to a stop in her powder-blue two tone Mercury, smiling brightly.

"I left Chuck and Kat in charge. I need to be back by four. It was a nice day for a drive."

Donovan climbed into the front seat. He folded his legs because Millie had the bench seat pulled forward to allow her feet to reach the pedals.

"Let's go to Listowel for lunch. I know a nice place." Millie dropped the clutch and sprayed gravel as she aimed the car onto the highway.

Maybe I can get a job in Goderich as a driving instructor. Donovan smiled. Millie dropped even further off the suspect list.

"I already ate your sandwich."

"You can eat again. You look a little skinny, probably cooking for yourself. I like my men on the plump side."

Snap!

She sped towards lunch. Donovan, full of ham sandwich wondered just how fat Millie liked her men.

About eleven in the evening, in the light of a three quarter gibbous moon, a semi-trailer backed through the gate beside the cattle pens. Bobby had aligned the freight car, so the open back of the trailer lined up nicely with the boxcar doorway. Three men got out of the cab and hurried to unload the furniture. Mike patted his chest, reassuring himself his snub-nosed.38 was ready. He would have preferred the heavy, long barrel RCMP issue, but his buster brown was back in his closet in Guelph, with an empty holster. The force had not allowed him to keep the gun. As a railway cop, he had thought he would never need a weapon for any more than scaring trespassers. To most people, a gun was a gun. If you were looking into the snout of a snub nose, it looked like a canon. In the hands of a good shooter, like Donovan, it was as deadly as any handgun.

The truck driver had killed the headlights but left the engine idling. Donovan crept up to record the details of the tractor, including the licence plate and name and address on the door. The moonlight was not his friend, and he hoped the men were too involved in the work to notice him creeping about in the semi-darkness. He listened. His ears strained through the sound of the diesel to make sure the three worked between the boxcar and the trailer. The occasional bump and curse re-assured.

The door sign was a hurried paint job. Paint had run under the stencil. The name was likely phoney. Maybe it had fake plates as well.

"I'm having a smoke," one man said.

Donovan heard boots crunch on the gravel and dove beneath the tractor unit, wiggling forward quickly to draw his legs well out of sight. A pair of boots walked to the cab door. He heard the man fumble inside for his smokes. Mike held his breath, face down on the gravel with his nose inches away from a pile of dried cattle dung. The .38 pressed against his chest. A glowing butt finally hit the ground beneath the driver's side running board. The smoker made a half-hearted attempt to quench the red ember with his boot before wandering to the rear to help finish the work.

Donovan eased from beneath the front bumper and scurried into the bush. The chairs he had pilfered came in handy. The men worked fast, and the truck pulled out about one in the morning. It was safer to be on the road than unloading a remote railway car in the middle of the night.

Mike was tired. It had been a long day. He brought Ed's railway Buick around to the cattle pen and put his stolen chairs into the car. At Maitland Station, he retrieved the key from behind the brick, stowed the chairs in the little used express shed and put Ed's keys back into the desk drawer. He thought about it. Ed had loaned him the car, but he could just as easily have taken it on his own.

"Who the hell are you?"

Donovan was locking the door, fumbling in the dark. He jumped at the surprise challenge and his hand went into his jacket to grip the handle of his .38. He turned towards the night man from the engine shed. The worker recognized him.

"I'm sorry, Mr Donovan. I saw the lights on and came to check. We've never had a problem here, but no one is here this time of the morning."

"No one ever comes around at night?"

"Nope... well, once in a while, Ed comes here. He did it one evening, a few weeks ago. He drove up in his car and went into the station. I never thought much of it. I had to get the ash box cleaned on 1232, so went back to work. When I looked out a few minutes later, the lights were out, and all was quiet. I guess he went right home. I also heard someone in the bunkhouse washroom."

"What night was that?"

"I think it was the night Blatchford had the accident. Maybe Ed got called out about it."

"What time was that?"

"About ten thirty. I come on at ten and was waiting for the firebox to cool."

"Are you sure it was, Ed?"

"Who else would it be? It was too dark, but it was his car. Sorry, I got to get back to the Pacific. Not much time after I cool her and clean the firebox to oil everything and relight her. Steam has to be up to two hundred in a few hours. I'll see you, Mr. Donovan." The night man disappeared.

Ed? I had him as a low level chance.

Donovan hid the key and headed to the hotel. It had been a useful but tiring day. He needed rest. Mike planned to go to the furniture factory and strong-arm Winslow to tell the truth.

18

Chapter Thirteen

Donovan walked by the Buick, giving it a long stare. It seemed to look different to him now that it seemed to be part of the story. It was mid-morning. He had slept in late. Millie had teased him over coffee.

"Hi Ed, thanks for lending me the car. Visiting my friend in Listowel would have been hard without it."

"Anytime, Donovan, it needs a good run now and then. I haven't even had it out of town for weeks."

Mike frowned.

"I'll take it up to the Supertest and fill it up later," Mike said. He took a seat on one of the dark oak passenger benches.

"I hope he's lowered his price. The last time I filled it was a doozie." Ed casually checked the drawer to make sure the keys were there.

"It won't matter to me. It was worth it. Thanks again."

Ed returned to update schedules with the trains back on their old times.

"Ed, did you get called down to the wreck that night?"

"No," he said.

Donovan noticed he did not seem to be surprised or worried.

"I was called about five in the morning to come early because of the coach and baggage car."

Donovan tried not to stare at the stationmaster. Was he lying? The story Mike heard last night seemed to put Ed near the top of the list, but he had little motive. The furniture thefts might be a reason, but we could accuse Ed at the most of not paying attention to train manifests and car movements. Mike doubted he could tie him into the thefts. That did not seem enough reason to kill.

The train crew, especially the front-end crew, was knees deep and everyone could go to jail.

O'Connell sat at the top of every list, including having two motives. He had Millie's car and Chuck's timing of Al's return to the hotel fit with the time Blatchford had died.

Perhaps the Buick had nothing to do with it and had its own innocent story. Or does it?

Mike thought some facts could fit another possibility. He adjusted his suspect list. Al was suddenly not alone at the top. Donovan did not like putting the names beneath O'Connell's. He settled in to wait for the afternoon manifest.

The clanging of the engine bell announced train 110. The Pacific eased past the station and Bobby jumped off. There were three boxcars between the tender and the grain cars. 315387 was the third boxcar. Bobby uncoupled the boxcars from the grain haulers, left them parked on the main and rode 315387 to the wye switch. He set the points, and they backed through the wye and onto the factory spur, disappearing into the trees towards the mill. Donovan waited. Fifteen minutes later, the Pacific appeared minus the boxcars.

***

Donovan walked calmly through the front door of Maitland Furniture and Woodworking. It was late afternoon. He had wanted to make sure they parked the mysterious boxcar at the factory.

"I would like to see Walter Winslow, please."

"Do you have an appointment?"

"I'm detective Donovan. I need to speak with Mr. Winslow." Mike flashed his badge. The woman did not ask which force Mike worked for. Technically, he had reduced jurisdiction off railway property, but that would not be an issue once he got past the gatekeeper. He was a sworn constable of The Crown, no matter who paid him.

Winslow appeared, "What do you want? You have no authority here."

"Is there a place we can talk privately?" Mike looked at the receptionist. She was all ears.

"I don't need to talk to you. You're a railway dick."

"One quick call and you'll have the OPP swarming all over here. Let's say I saw some interesting things yesterday and last night."

Winslow went white. "Come with me." He glanced back at the receptionist. The woman suddenly found some paperwork to do. Her eyes followed them, peeking beneath her lids as the men headed to the back. She had known for months there was something fishy going on. The woman typed all the shipping manifests, except once a month, Winslow wrote one. Once she recovered from the insult, she had realized something probably illegal was going on. She was glad not to be part of it.

Winslow thought the railway loading dock was the most private. Donovan liked the fact that 315387 sat in sight to drive home his points. He also thought Winslow had a gun somewhere on the premises. Mike gambled Winslow did not have it on him or would be crazy enough to shoot a cop while surrounded by witnesses.

"I'm not beating around the bush, Winslow. I know everything about your little theft operation here and could get you behind bars in an hour. You lied to me the other day about knowing Blatchford and O'Connell. I want the truth. At the moment, your crimes," Mike emphasized the word 'crimes', are less interesting than Blatchford's murder."

"Murder?" Winslow seemed shocked. Donovan pounced.

"Yes, someone murdered him. You aren't high on the suspect list, but you had a motive. Blatchford poked around about that boxcar." Donovan nodded up at the siding.

"If I have to call in the OPP, suspicion of murder might be on your head besides theft."

"What do you want?" Winslow shook.

"You lied about meeting Blatchford. Tell me about it. I want the truth."

"Yah, he came up here one day with that little tramp from the hotel." Mike frowned. "If I want a character reference for anyone, Winslow, it won't be from you. Stick to the facts."

"Blatchford nosed around the boxcar," Winslow glanced up the track. "I ran him off, told him it was none of his business. They went over to the river for a bit and then left."

"I said the truth." Donovan crossed his arms. He had a good foot and fifty pounds on Winslow. The little man shrank back.

"That is the truth."

Mike sighed. "What about your gun?"

"I don't have a gun."

"Do you have a phone I can use?" Mike headed for the door.

"Okay, okay, I had a gun, but I don't have it anymore."

"Someone saw you following Blatchford and the girl with a snub-nosed revolver. Stop sandbagging. Tell me everything. Make it good."

"I followed them to the river. I was going to shoot Blatchford, but chickened out. He and the girl were naked." Winslow said it as if God was about to strike him down for looking. "I came back here and then they came out and left."

"I guess you didn't stick around over there getting an eye full?"

"Well, uh, yes, I..." Winslow could not admit his voyeurism.

"Was that it?" Donovan thought perhaps it was, but Winslow surprised him. The man thought Donovan knew it all and was ready to send him to jail if he held back.

"I went to corner him at the station that night. I offered not to tell Millie about her wanton... about her daughter if Blatchford forgot about the boxcar. He laughed at me. Everyone laughs at me. I pulled my gun on him. I might have shot him right there, but he tricked me, knocked me down and took the gun. Some of Al's guys came along, so I drove off. Blatchford got the gun."

Donovan made some notes.

"Blatchford kept the gun?"

"Yes, the bastard."

"You lied to me about O'Connell, too. He was in on the entire operation. You two knew each other well."

Again Winslow thought Mike talked from facts, not guesswork.

"Yah, we saw each other a lot."

"He came up here to see you the night Blatchford died."

"Yes, a bit after nine. He asked to meet me at nine, but was late. He wanted to stop the thefts. I told him we were dealing with some bad dudes and the boss had to make at least one more shipment yesterday's load. I told him that would be it, but I wasn't sure the boss could do that. The punks we are selling to scare me." Winslow paused and then said, "I swear I didn't know the girl was Al's daughter. I didn't know Al knew I'd been watching them. He laid a good one on my chin before he left, knocked me down and then spun his wheels to spray me with gravel as he pulled out. That guy could do anything."

"Where were you before you met with Al?"

"I was home. My wife will tell you that. I left about half-past eight, partway through Dinah Shore. I told her I had some work to do."

Donovan added the comment to his notes.

"Two pieces of advice, Winslow, tell your boss to end the scheme. I don't know what I'm going to do about it, but if someone annoys me, I'll collar you all. The other thing, don't buy another gun. Guns are dangerous and you aren't the Lone Ranger."

Mike headed back to the station in the Buick.

Now there's another loose end. What the hell did Blatchford do with the gun?

Mike had searched all of Blatchford's belongings in Goderich, and he did not see a gun in the wreck. He would ask Bowers to search around where the wreck had happened. There was not much hope. The track crew had disturbed much of the area. If one of them found a gun, they probably stole it. It was unlikely that it would have flown out of the cab.

The gun seemed to be important. It might change things. Blatchford knew many people were out to get him. The gun might have seemed like a gift. The man had been in the army. He knew about guns. If he had the pistol on him that night, he might have tried to pull it on the killer before they hit him. Donovan did not know if Blatchford was a guy who could shoot someone close-up. Mike knew, looking someone in the eye and squeezing the trigger was a hard thing to do.

Mike wrote, *the killer might have the gun* into the notebook.

"You should reward frequent customers." Mike said to the gas station owner as he paid for the fill-up.

"I do," he laughed. "You get to see my smile more." The man took the two-dollar bill.

Donovan returned the Buick to the station.

"You're getting to be a regular." Harold sat beside Mike as the coach on train 101 sped along towards Elmira.

"I'll ask the president for a private car." They laughed.

"Every time I think I'm getting somewhere, something new comes up. You will see me tonight, too."

"I see you like Millie's cooking."

"Everything is tempting," Mike agreed.

Mike sat in the railway police car, watching Irene Blatchford's house half a block away. The Plymouth was in the driveway, but he had checked the spare board when he had arrived. It scheduled Jones to report at eleven. At ten forty-five, Irene and Jones came out and drove off in the car without paying attention to the street. Mike waited. Irene was still in her housecoat and would likely be right back. On cue, at five past eleven, the Plymouth arrived in the driveway. Donovan let Irene have ten minutes to settle. He hoped she had dressed. He knocked.

"Bill never brought a gun home." Irene smiled at Mike, who was sipping a steaming cup of Bokar coffee.

"Does George have a gun?"

"Not that I know of. Should I be afraid of George? Will you protect me?" Her smile became seductive. "I bet you have a big gun."

She's watching too many movies.

Irene rose to fetch more coffee. She had changed into a tight blouse and a form fitting skirt. "I never used to like cops before now." When she returned with the top button on her blouse undone.

"I am a little afraid now."

"Maybe I can help you there," Mike said, "once this is all over."

I had better get out of here. She's a charmer.

"Did George do it?" she hugged him at the door. For all of her forwardness, she seemed to be patient. Irene played the game well.

"I'm sure he didn't. I'll see you soon." Mike squeezed her hand and headed to the station. Blatchford's locker had no secrets and no gun.

Mike rode Train-100 all the way to Goderich. He wanted to search the bunkhouse. That night, Jones was the fireman/brakeman on the RS1. The CSR and the union were just beginning a long fight over what to call, and what to pay the second man in a diesel locomotive. The railway wanted to do away with the second man altogether. George showed Donovan where Blatchford had bunked. There was no sign of the gun. Mike did not think Bill would have hidden it there anyway, but he had to be thorough. He tracked down Chief Bowers and hitched a ride back to Maitland.

"They did not shoot him. I don't see why the gun is important."

"Maybe it isn't." Mike leaned in the driver's window before going into Millie's. His jacket rode a little high, revealing the snug slacks on his buttocks. Two high school girls walking home along the far side of the street whistled and laughed.

Times have sure changed, thought Donovan. *It was the war.*

"I have a hunch the killer has the gun. Blatchford took it from Winslow, and the killer took the gun from Blatchford after he hit him."

"Why were Blatchford and Winslow fighting?" Bowers was as smart as Donovan had pegged him to be.

"Over Kathleen, I think. Winslow was trying to blackmail Blatchford." Donovan wanted to keep the furniture stealing out of it. Perhaps it would be the motive, but he was not sure he wanted to lower the hammer on a bunch of bit players in a scheme where almost no one lost. The murder was the important case.

Why do people do stupid things?

"Millie, I want to search Al's room."

She had cleared breakfast away. Mike and Millie were having a second cup of coffee. The dining room was empty.

"What are you looking for?"

"A gun Blatchford took from Winslow. It's missing."

"It wouldn't be good if Al had a gun when he's drunk," Millie said. "I'll let you in."

Al had not attempted to hide the snub nosed .38. It was in the top drawer of his nightstand, on top of two crisp fifty-dollar bills, the kickback from the last shipment.

"Does this mean Al did it?"

"I'm guessing that it's Winslow's pea shooter." Mike laughed as he removed the bullets. His own sidearm was about the same. "It makes it look bad for Al." He squinted at the serial number. "I'll get the OPP to check this number, but I bet it has been illegal for a long time, probably smuggled from Detroit. I doubt I can attach Winslow's name, or Al's."

"I'm scared," Millie shuddered. "Al can be violent, but the only weapon I ever saw him use was a beer bottle, and he just threatened with it."

"He might have a good explanation." Mike wanted to reassure Millie. "There are others who could have done it. Others I didn't really suspect before. I'll know this afternoon."

Donovan was just finishing his lunch. Millie was fussing at the cash register, keeping one eye on the detective. She was wondering if she had been sleeping with a murderer. She was wondering if Mike was thinking about that. The phone rang.

"The call's for you, from Guelph, some woman named Irene," Millie frowned. "I'll leave."

"No, stay," Donovan smiled. There are too many secrets around here as it is. "I'll just be a minute."

"Mr. Donovan, Mike, should I be afraid of George? He wants to take me to dinner, to help take my mind off Bill's death. Will I be safe?" Her tone was coy. "Do I need protection?"

"George is a good man, Irene. You should be okay for a meal at least. The rest is up to you."

"Thank you, Mike. I always feel safe with you." Mike was not sure if he heard a blown kiss.

"I'll see you when I'm in town." They said goodbyes.

Mike withdrew in thought.

"Girlfriend?" Millie pried.

"What? Oh, no," Donovan winked and even though he did not believe it, said, "half a suspect, Blatchford's widow."

"Good." Millie left for the kitchen. Mike sighed deeply.

What was it they said about me in the yearbook, 'Mike Donovan, the guy least likely to get his girl but most likely to get his man?'

His classmates knew about Donovan's childhood ambition to be a Mountie. Mike had little luck with girls back then. He had liked that pretty dark-haired girl, Maria Ferraro. She teased him mercilessly at school. Mike thought she liked him too, but they had no future. Her father never allowed Maria off the porch, except to go to school or church.

Once, when he and Maria had been studying together in the kitchen, her father had arrived home from work.

"So you like Maria," Mr. Farraro had said in his old country accent. "She's a good girl."

When a man who grew up in Calabria said something like that, smart young schoolboys knew what he meant.

***

A major storm passed just to the south of Maitland Station. Mike sat in the station's gloom, sipping Chuck's coffee and watching sheets of rain, highlighted by bright flashes, pounding onto the rail yard. The Pacific rolled by on the lead track. The crew went about the job of re-arranging the train before heading to Goderich. Bobby suffered in the rain, but it halted and the sun shone, drying him in the fifteen minutes it took to drop cars onto the stubs.

Mike went out the door onto the Maitland Station platform and walked to where the Pacific would come to a stop as it coupled to the parked train. They had split a few cars of coal and lumber away from 110 at Maitland. Bobby hung onto the back ladder of the tender. Donovan saw mist rising from his clothes as the sun warmed him. O'Connell eased the knuckles together as if he were a surgeon. Bobby jumped off to check the knuckle and join the airline. Donovan climbed into the cab of 1232.

"Can I get a ride to Goderich?"

"Don't get in the way," grunted O'Connell. He had noticed Millie's flirting.

"You can stand behind me once Bobby's back on." Walter smiled. "You finished your investigation yet?"

"Just about," said Donovan. He looked at a toolbox resting on the far side of the coal chute.

"Who's toolbox is that?"

"It's Bobby's," O'Connell said, "in case a switch sticks or a knuckle is stubborn. It happens a lot, especially in winter."

Donovan could see a wrench identical to the murder weapon. He had seen Bobby swing that wrench to free the switch arm at the cattle siding.

"What's Bobby like?"

"He'll never amount to much," Al gave his longstanding opinion.

"He's a nice kid," said Walter. "He's planning to take care of his sister as soon as he gets more pay. That's why he wants the diesel ticket so bad."

"Humph," grunted Al.

"His father's a drunken abuser. Bobby wants to get Roberta out of the house first, and then the rest of them. He's desperate for that."

Bobby climbed on board. Donovan said nothing. He had never felt less eager to collar a criminal in his policing career. Everyone in the cab seemed to be nervous. Walter shoveled more coal than necessary and then leaned on his shovel, staring past O'Connell out into the sunny farmland. Al blew a little louder and longer than normal at each crossing. Bobby sat in the fireman's chair and stared through sunglasses at his side of the track, as if expecting a broken rail to appear. Mike hung onto a stanchion as the cab pitched back and forth. Donovan felt the tension that he caused.

The Goderich sub was in decline and the track was not receiving the attention it needed. As they approached the Highway 21 fly over in what passed for silence in a steam locomotive cab, Mike pulled Winslow's pistol from his pocket.

"Does anyone recognize this?"

Bobby and Al looked horrified.

"Is that what killed Blatchford?" Al asked. He knew where Donovan had found it.

"They hit him on the head," says Bobby. "What's the gun for?"

"Whoever had this gun killed Blatchford and took it off the dead body." He looked at Al. "I found it in your room."

"I didn't kill him. I got it from Bobby. He showed me the gun. He said he found it and wondered if I knew someone who would buy it. I told Bobby I knew a motorcycle punk in Guelph who would probably give fifty for it. I was going to see him on the weekend." Al had realized the implications and sounded nervous. He stared at Bobby.

Donovan had already decided Al was innocent. The Buick the night-man saw return to the station and the lack of skid marks took the suspicion from O'Connell.

"I know what a street gun goes for. He would have paid a hundred. You were going to rip Bobby off."

"Bastard!" Everyone turned to Bobby.

"How did you know they hit him on the head, Bobby? Was it because of this?"

Donovan pulled the large wrench from the toolbox.

"Nice tools you have there, Bobby. This looks very handy. Only Chief Bowers and I knew one of these clobbered Blatchford."

Walter seemed puzzled. Bobby looked scared. O'Connell throttled back, slowing into Meneset station on the downslope to the Maitland bridge. Donovan was now sure.

"Want to tell me about it, son?" Donovan stared into Bobby's eyes. There was a long minute of silence as anguish filled Bobby's face. Donovan waited.

Bobby cried. Tears formed lines down his soot smudged face.

"I didn't want to do it. I didn't see any choice."

"Do what?" Donovan swung the wrench casually.

"I killed Blatchford. He had it coming, messing with our business. He would have put us in jail just to get to drive on the main line. Everyone wanted him dead. I nearly didn't have the guts."

"What happened?" Donovan grasped the tool, but relaxed against the bulkhead. He had temporarily forgotten about his nice tweed jacket.

"He knew about the boxcar we were dropping with the stolen furniture."

"Shut up, you stupid pup." Al stood and let go of the throttle. He took a step towards Bobby. Donovan stepped between them and stared Al down.

"I know all about it," Mike said. "I don't even need Bobby's statement as proof." Donovan turned back to the young man.

"He was going to tell. I asked him not to tell. So did the guy at the factory. It was no use. He laughed at me, called me stupid. My life would have been over, no job, prison. I'd never work again. Roberta would never... I had to kill him. He was a jerk anyway."

"How did you do it?"

"I thought I planned it so well. Everyone would think it was an accident. I'd stop the train at Meneset, unhook the coaches so no one else got hurt, clobber Jones and Blatchford, and then make sure the train wrecked. I thought at high speed it would roll off at the bridge and end up in the river."

"Maybe if you had set it to the eighth notch, it would have. You left it at five."

"So that's why. I couldn't figure out what I did wrong, along with the problem I had with Jones."

"Yes," Mike said. "Jones being found at Meneset was puzzling, part of why I thought it was more than an accident."

"He was supposed to be in the cab with Blatchford. He must have heard me pulling the knuckle pin. They set the RS3 up with the short hood to the rear. He must have heard me. Jones was coming out of the cab door by the time I got there. I had to hit him, but after the first blow, he went head first over the catwalk rail and rolled down the hill. He probably recognized me."

"Maybe he did," Donovan said, "but he can't remember anything that happened after Bill got off at Meneset."

"I hoped he was dead, but I didn't have the time to go looking for him or have the strength to put him onto the engine. Blatchford was already coming back."

"I clobbered Blatchford, hit him three times to make sure, and lifted him into the engineer's seat. The gun fell out of his hand. He was going to shoot me. I took it. I had the half-baked idea I would go find Jones and shoot him. Then I set the wrench to hold down the dead man, took off the brakes, blew the horn twice like starting up and then set one notch. As soon as she rolled, I pushed the throttle up to set it to eight.

I guess I panicked and didn't notice. I ran out the fireman's door and went off the back step and hit the ground on the wrong foot. The engine was moving pretty good then, and I pitched forward. No one noticed my bruises, but I hit hard and sprained an ankle a bit. It took me a minute to catch my breath. I forgot about my idea of going after Jones with my ankle like that, so I took off up the hill to the car. My foot was hurting all the way. I drove around a little and parked to calm down."

"You got back about ten thirty?"

"Yes, about then. I showered when I got back to Maitland and ran some cold water on my foot. By morning, it was good."

The train carried around the curve approaching Meneset. Al applied some brake and searched ahead for the semaphore.

"How did you get to Meneset? Where did you get a car?"

"I borrowed Ed's Buick. He was gone home. He always leaves the station key behind the window brick. I saw him do that, and his car keys were in his desk drawer. It was easy. Nice car too. I never owned a car."

Donovan smiled. It confirmed his guesswork at the parking lot.

"I made sure I headed back to the bunkhouse from the hotel before Train 100 went through. The guys came with me, but I had an excuse all set for Walter. I didn't need one. He went to get his stuff. I shut my bunk room door and slipped out behind the parked boxcars and over to the station."

Walter nodded. "I thought he was asleep."

As usual, they set the Meneset semaphore to medium clear. Al let the train run through, listening to Bobby's story.

The kid's smarter and braver than I thought. Too bad he's caught. Now we're all caught. Donovan was smarter than all of us.

Al's heart was growing heavier with each wheel click on a track joint. When they got to the Goderich station, Donovan would arrest them all, Bobby for murder, he and Walter for helping steal the furniture. If nothing else, the railway would fire them for misuse of CSR property.

"So you got here," Donovan nodded out the window at the passing Meneset station building, "and set the signals to stop."

"Yes, that was easy. Every once in a while there's a stop signal telling the engineer to wait and call Goderich."

"It's first degree," said Al. "If Bobby goes to trial the motive, the furniture stuff will come out. We'll all go down with him. He'll hang and we'll end up in jail." Al looked at Edwards.

The Pacific was approaching the river. Sunlight and shadow flickered as they ran through the trees. Al eased off to the second notch for the shallow curve to line up the bridge.

Maybe I should stop in the middle of the bridge and throw Donovan into the river. Al eased the throttle back to the first notch, wondering if Walter would go along with killing the cop.

"A jury might not hang him after they hear the complete story." Donovan knew vengeance was now less of a motivation with courts. There was even talk of doing away with hanging.

Al tried to signal Edwards about pitching Donovan into the river. Walter turned away.

"I guess we're done for." Al hoped Walter might change his mind.

"It was a brilliant plan. I would have gotten away with it too, but..."

Suddenly, Bobby grabbed the brake handle and threw it to full emergency. He jumped off before the engine had stopped. This time, he landed on the right foot and ran. The fascinating story had lulled Donovan, and he was a few seconds slow in following.

The engine hissed to a stop a few yards from the bridge. Loud banging ran back along the train like an echoing gunshot as each trailing coupling lost its slack.

Bobby was already fifty feet onto the structure. Donovan did not have his gun. Blatchford's weapon was in his pocket, but he had taken the bullets out. He would never have shot the man. He had never fired while on duty, although he had threatened to shoot once. Shooting a man in the back, even a fleeing murderer, was the method of gangsters, not cops.

Mike began the perilous run across the bridge. There was no centre plank walkway. Big openings revealed the river far below. The ties were damp and slippery from the earlier storm. Afternoon sun on the rivulets in the water flashed between each tie. It was hard to look down to find sure footing. His leather shoes didn't give him good traction. Mike had to pay close attention to each step. He was in good condition and keeping pace with Bobby, who had the same problems. Behind him, Al blasted the steam whistle continuously, the standard railway signal for trouble. A dozen anglers up and down the river stared incomprehensibly at the black, steaming Pacific wailing at the end of the bridge.

"Bobby, stop," Donovan cried out. "You won't get away, anyway."

Damn! Donovan's hat flew off. He hoped it stayed on the bridge.

At the sound of Mike's voice, Bobby turned, checking the distance. Two more steps. His foot caught between two ties and he sprawled between the rails. The cop was closing fast. Bobby jumped up and ran hard. He made the mistake of looking back again, and this time a toe caught the edge of a tie, throwing him sideways.

It seemed to be so sudden to Donovan. One instant Bobby was looking at him in fear, the next his body flew over the downstream side of the bridge. The terrified scream sickened Donovan as Bobby fell. It sounded like he had called out to *Roberta*. It only took three seconds. He landed in about a foot of water, head first, and the shallow bottom instantly broke his neck. Mike came to a sudden stop, nearly lost his footing and, for an instant, thought he might join Bobby in the river. He glimpsed water flashing back and forth past the edge of the bridge before regaining his balance.

At a slower pace, his chest heaving, Donovan approached the spot and looked over. The body was floating gently in the backwater beside a pier. A man who had been fishing on the far shore was splashing through the water and soon had hold of Bobby.

"Is he dead?" Donovan shouted.

"I think so," a shaky voice replied.

Donovan stepped onto the safety platform and signalled for Al to come ahead. The whistle mercifully stopped. With bell clanging, the Pacific rolled slowly over the bridge.

"Go down to the station and call the cops. Send an ambulance. Bobby's dead, according to a guy with him in the water."

"Crazy, Bobby went nuts." Donovan shouted the explanation to Milt as the caboose eased past Donovan's uneasy perch on the narrow platform. The conductor had been walking up the train to investigate the emergency stop and the danger signal. He had grabbed the handrail as the caboose caught up to him and was now hanging off the bottom step.

Mike found his hat jammed between two ties. He slowly followed the train over the bridge. At the spot where Bobby had fallen, he found sunglasses. They were military pilot style. Donovan stared at them for a minute. The last two men who had worn these glasses were dead. He threw them as far as he could into the river. Sirens were growing louder on North Harbour Road.

The fisherman had already dragged Bobby's body to shore. Mike tore his grey flannel slacks in the brambles and his shoes were muddy and scraped. He could not think of them. Of all the suspects who had still been on Donovan's list, of the five in O'Connell's crew, Bobby was the last one he had wanted to condemn.

19

Chapter Fourteen

"**B**owers, the local cop is coming here in a few minutes. He knows nothing about the boxcar. Keep it that way."

Donovan had gathered all the remaining crew of train 110. They were standing beside the Pacific, parked on the lead opposite the station. Train 100 was due in a half hour.

"Bowers will want to talk to everyone. You two, Mike turned to Al and George, tell him Bobby confessed to the murder just like he said. Say he had some personal hate for Blatchford. Tell him Bobby was fooling around with Blatchford's wife and wanted her for himself."

"Why are you doing this?" Al lacked his usual aggressive pose. He stood like a contrite schoolboy.

"I'm not doing it for you, O'Connell. You're an idiot getting involved in this scheme. You're all idiots." Donovan fixed them with a scowl.

"How much were you all getting? Was it a hundred for you, Al? Not much, I'd guess, and risking your futures. Blatchford's murder only got me here sooner. Eventually someone would have noticed that phoney car number, and I would have been here, and it wouldn't have been hard to figure out. I would have had to jail you all."

All the men shrank at Donovan's scolding.

"We'll talk about that tomorrow afternoon when you're done with your run. The four of you go to Millie's. I'm going to save your ass ends."

Donovan walked away, leaving a developing confrontation behind. "You're getting a hundred, Al? You two-faced tight ass..." Mike smiled. The little gang on the Pacific run would forever be fighting. Their punishment had just begun. He doubted they would share a beer together again after tomorrow.

Bowers appeared after taking care of Bobby's body and arranging for an autopsy. He had finished interviewing the shaken angler. Donovan tried to ignore his smudged jacked and dirty, torn pants as he crossed the tracks to the platform and approached the chief.

"Richard, come for a walk." Donovan escorted Chief Bowers some distance away from the station along the repaired main stub that now sat empty. It was a pleasant evening after the earlier storm. The beauty of the setting sun contrasted with the dark tragedy of Bobby Ellis' death.

"Bobby dying was an accident. He went crazy and jumped out of the engine after confessing to killing Blatchford. He ran over the bridge and fell by accident. Write it up the way it happened. It's the complete story. I'll sign a statement."

"Is this another fallen tree, Donovan?" Bowers was skeptical. "Can I guess there's more to this?"

"You can guess," Mike said, "but as you know, guesses aren't evidence."

"How do I close the Blatchford file? The OPP CID will ask questions. They don't trust us small town cops."

"We'll make sure your report is neat, and all tied up. I don't feel bad about the CSR and the insurance company paying up, no matter what Blatchford was like as a person. His widow deserves the money. If it had been suicide, Irene Blatchford wouldn't get anything."

Donovan knew Irene's attractiveness partly motivated him, but she would never tempt him. At his age, if he was to get hooked up with a woman, it would be one who only wanted him, and as much as he would only want her. He wanted a quiet life and not a high maintenance woman. An independent one, sure of herself, and willing to put up with this habitual bachelor who sometimes liked to wander off into the woods to sit on a damp log and rest his mind would be the only one. Someone who was at least as good a cook as Mike Donovan; someone like... Reality interrupted his dreaming.

"It doesn't even matter. Jones will probably benefit from all of this. George took quite a blow on the head and Bobby would have killed him too, if he hadn't fallen off the engine. He was innocent of everything but bedding Irene Blatchford. That's not a crime; that's for sure. I don't think he had to work hard to seduce her. In the end, he'll get the girl. The real loser seems to be Bobby's sister, Roberta, and the rest of his family. I'm going to look into that when I get back to Guelph. I hate wife-beaters."

"I'm actually glad it was murder. I've spent a lot of CSR money and they wouldn't like it if I didn't have results. My boss is an accountant, not a cop, and he'll love having a nice thick report to file away."

Donovan looked over at the station. O'Connell and Edwards were sitting on a bench in shock. The two men did not yet believe they were being spared going to jail. They eyed Donovan as if he were a dangerous animal with fangs and claws, ready to turn on them.

"You'll have to talk to the crew." Mike nodded towards the station.

"Only Edwards and O'Connell were there and heard the confession. Take it easy on them. They're shaken up badly. The two in the caboose saw nothing. I'll talk to them, but I think we can leave them out of it."

"Are you a judge?" Bowers was serious.

"Let's just say I'm for justice. In the end there are two dead men, one of them a killed the other and only some federal tax dollars missing. Maybe it'll keep them from taking one Indian kid."

Donovan puzzled Bowers, but the chief said nothing. He did not see how taxes and Indian kids figured into it all. Donovan was now his friend, even if he was strange, for a cop. He knew Mike had to be referring to something from his life as a Mountie and some aspect of this case he had not revealed. Bowers would never know how the boxcar and the thievery led to the tragedy.

"There are lots of loose ends. If anyone's asking, what do I put in the report?" Bowers looked worried. "What was his motive?"

"Jones wasn't the only one in Irene's bed." Donovan repeated the lie he had told the engine crew to use. "It was the classic lover wanting the woman. She's a hot piece, if you know what I mean. Just like in a movie. I think that's where the kid got the idea. He wasn't too bright. He intended to kill Jones, too. Eliminate everyone wanting Irene Blatchford."

"Maybe Mrs. Blatchford was in on it," Bowers again saw himself as Broderick Crawford. "Maybe she asked Bobby to do it."

"No, Blatchford was her meal ticket. She was getting all the sex she needed on the side for free. Bobby wanted to make more money. Blatchford found out about Bobby and his wife and told him he would tell the CSR Bobby was no good as an engineer. He wanted to screw up the kid's future for revenge."

"That kind of thing could be more common than you think." Bowers said.

Donovan had no regrets about putting a smudge on Irene's reputation. He knew first hand she could have several lovers. She was attractive, but Bowers would never meet her. It was unlikely she and Donovan would ever cross paths again, unless she went back to work at the Guelph railway lunch counter. That would not happen if she stuck with Jones.

"Call me when you're done, and I'll come down and sign my statement. I'd like to review the file to see if I missed anything and make sure the OPP won't have questions. There is a notebook in the hotel. I'll give that to you then."

Donovan wanted to check the file to make sure it did not mention the boxcar. He had the notebook in his pocket, but wasn't yet ready to let Bowers have it. Bowers spent ten minutes with Al and Walter and then went back to town to write his report, giving them the usual line of being ready to be interviewed again if necessary.

Train 100 arrived. Donovan boarded the Pacific with Al and Walter. They had the empty grain cars and two road graders on flats ready to roll.

Mike tore the pages that mentioned 315387 out of Blatchford's notebook.

"What are those?" Walter asked.

"Open the firebox," Mike ignored Edwards.

Donovan crumpled the paper into a tight little ball and confined the secret of boxcar 315387 to the inferno of the Pacific's boiler.

20

Chapter fifteen

Mike slapped the thick file onto one of Millie's dining room tables and sat. All of Al O'Connell's crew were present, save for the spare brakeman who replaced Bobby. They left the new man on the Pacific, keeping the boiler hot. Kathleen and Millie sat off to Mike's right.

"What's that?" Al asked?

"My report," Mike said, "of the strange comings and goings of boxcar 315387."

He opened the folder and stared at the contents.

"You don't deserve it, but I'm going to keep you all working and out of jail." He did not include the women in his scowling look.

"What I'm going to do is, let's say, irregular. Officially, this boxcar investigation doesn't exist. The CSR has never heard of this. Unless one of you convinces me otherwise, it's going to stay that way. I'm taking a risk, but I'm depending on honour among thieves that you'll keep your mouths shut. If you don't, this report becomes official. I'd need to cover my ass too." Donovan smiled.

"What if we grab that file and burn it? Then you got nothing." Al sounded as if he was ready to do it. Mike did not flinch. Behind him, Millie smirked, wishing she had her brass curtain rod handy. She was getting used to the idea of clobbering railway engineers.

"This isn't the only copy." He taunted O'Connell with a grin. "I'm a cop, but not a stupid cop. Did you know the drug store will make duplicates of your photos for fifty cents? It's amazing. The mimeograph machine is a modern wonder. The duplicate is at my desk in Guelph."

Mike lied. It was in his luggage upstairs. There had been no time to get to Guelph. He pulled out a photo.

"Here's a nice shot of Bobby hanging from the boxcar at Mile 47." He picked up another. "One of you, Walter, watching from the Pacific. None of you, Al, sorry, but I'm sure Walter will testify under oath that you were running the train that day."

O'Connell flashed a dark look at Edwards. Mike knew things might be a little tense in the cab until Al retired in the spring.

"Here are some nice ones of a boxcar with 315387 written on it. De-lightful pictures and more of furniture inside." He admired his camera skills. "That number should be actually running pulpwood into Espanola. Ed, you should have known the number was wrong, if you had been doing your job and watching the manifests and the yard. I assume you got a few bucks to look the other way. You didn't tell me Blatchford was looking at your files and you had a bit of a set to. Understandable, a thief doesn't tell a cop they are a thief." Ed squirmed.

"I wish I could do more to have you make up for your stupidity. Up north, the Cree would have you doing the equivalent of track work once a week for a month for stealing from the community. I can't do that. Just make you squirm."

"It was bad enough for you to watch a friend die, even if he was a murderer. He wouldn't have been a murderer if it wasn't for you all. I'll have to be content with that. You'll have to live with that. In fact, he might have been better than you all. He just wanted to save his sister. Live with knowing it was your stupidity that made him do it." Mike paused.

"Perhaps you're all guilty and I should turn you in."

Everyone gasped. O'Connell stood, about to pounce.

"Sit, Al!" Millie ordered and reached for her heavy glass ashtray. Al sat.

"I'm not going to nab you. I'm going to spare you all. Winslow and whoever was helping him at the factory were the actual thieves. One day they'll pay. The last shipment showed up short. Maybe the customer will deal with them."

"It's Winslow and the owner," Al chirped in. "The owner was the guy who organized it all. He was stealing from himself. It looked like easy money to us."

"There's no free lunch," Donovan replied. "But you have to buy your stay out of jail free card. You're all going to take the money you got for this and give it to Millie."

"I don't want it. Why would you do that?" For an instant, she thought Donovan was trying to impress her, maybe buy her. It would not happen.

I shouldn't have told him the story of the hotel.

"Don't worry, Millie," Donovan caught her anger. "This isn't a free ride for you. You ignored it all, so you are responsible. Your contribution is to take in Bobby's sister, Roberta. Bobby died because he was desperate to get her away from their father before he raped her. I've talked to her on the phone and will settle it all when I go to Bobby's funeral. The money is to help cover her expenses at the start. I can see you needing extra help here soon."

Millie could not read Donovan's smile.

"But I don't need more help."

"You will." Donovan adjusted his tie and blushed slightly. Only Millie caught it.

"Ed, you have railway red paint in the yard, and white. Al's crew is going to get 315387 from the factory and park it in the engine shed. One of you paints out that damned three and paint number one back where it belongs. I've sent Chuck to the Canadian Tire in Goderich. He's getting a few cans of that new spray-on paint. I told him to get a few pleasant colours," Donovan chuckled. No one understood what he was talking about.

"Any of you guys artists?"

"I like to paint," Kat spoke, confused by the talk about theft and jail. She had known nothing about the boxcar. "I got all A's in school."

"Thanks," Mike smiled, "I'm turning you into a juvenile delinquent. You're going to go into the shed tomorrow and vandalize the boxcar. Use the spray cans to make some interesting designs above the numbers and CSR lettering on both sides of the boxcar. Make it nice and make sure you cover up the logo and most of the numbers. Have fun." He smiled again.

"Do you get along with Henry on 6275?" Mike asked Al. "You don't get along with too many people."

"Yah, he's okay." Al was a delightful shade of Irish red with the freckles on his face, competing with the age mottles and red beer-nose.

"Good. Tomorrow afternoon, when you get back here with 110, take the boxcar from the shed and haul it to Goderich with you. There's a crossover from CSR to the CNR track at the grain elevators. Have Henry stick it onto that little CN stub on the far side of their yard. They have some dead looking rolling stock on there as it is. You guys will have to decide how to bribe Henry and the CN switcher. A two-four or a bottle of rye seems to be the currency for bribery. Eventually, someone at CN will try to figure out the car, and it'll wander back to the CSR. Al, I think you'll be retired by then. Now, go get that boxcar."

The train crew left. Donovan went upstairs for a nap before dinner. It had been an exhausting several days, both physically and emotionally. There was no handy spruce forest to go wandering in for relief, and no Billy Pyne to repeat his old, old stories.

There was a light knock on his door at dinnertime.

"Mike... dinner," Millie's voice was soft.

Donovan opened the door. Millie stood, wanting to push him back in and shut the door, wanting to drag him into her room, wanting... she did not know what.

"Thank you," she said instead. They went down to dinner.

***

Early the next morning, Kat disappeared into the engine shed. It took her until lunchtime to finish the job. She returned, smiling.

"What did you paint?" Donovan was curious.

"You'll see." Donovan thought she smiled too much. She and Chuck kept looking at Mike and grinned throughout lunch. When O'Connell and 110 arrived, Mike, Chuck and Kat piled into the Olds and headed to Goderich station. Donovan wanted to be sure that everything had happened as planned. Chuck and Kat wanted to watch Donovan.

They sat in the shade of the platform overhang, sipping Cokes. Donovan told a few of what he hoped were interesting stories from his time on the Mounties. It had become important to him that Kat like him.

At last, the manifest arrived with the errant boxcar coupled behind the Pacific's tender. They dropped the caboose and crept past the station on the lead track. Donovan was in disbelief. Kat peeked at him from the corner of her eye, giggling.

She had covered the CSR logo with a fairly well drawn cartoon of a Mountie in red surge and a Stetson hat. A hint of orange hair peeked out under the hat. He had googly eyes that stared back at anyone looking. The character had one foot on a stump and one hand held a black steel skillet. Wavy blue lines of water covered the car number below. A grey fish peeked out with a grin. Between the water and the Mountie were the words, *The Mountie always gets his pan.* Kat and Chuck went into hysterics. Donovan broke into a grin.

"It isn't Nelson Eddy, but it'll do. You really are delinquent. I'd better speak to your momma." He could not muster a frown. "You might start a whole new art movement."

"Not in this little town," Kat managed through her giggles. "Maybe I should move to New York. Momma would love you to talk to her."

She winked.

"What's that?" Jenkins, the stationmaster, had come out to watch the spectacle.

"It came up from Guelph. I think it's for Goderich's hundred and thirtieth celebration." Mike sounded like he believed it.

"Maybe we should park it on the stub where the wreck was. It would draw a crowd." Jenkins returned to his office.

Henry seemed embarrassed as he moved the colourful boxcar into the obscure siding.

"Chuck, just how much paint did you buy?" Donovan had not looked at the receipt.

"About two dozen cans. The nosey Parker at the counter asked me what I wanted all that for. I said Millie was going to do a new sign for the hotel, Millie and Mike's."

"Are you *sure* that doctor didn't drop you on your head?" Mike said, but his blush raised his freckles to new glory.

***

"Al seems to keep a low profile." Donovan noted the engineer was not in his usual dinner spot at Millie's table. Tonight it was only Millie, Mike, Kat, and Chuck.

"I threw him out," Millie said. "I told him he nearly got us all in jail. He'd never been a father to Kat." She smiled at Kathleen. "He was just using me. I should have done it years ago."

Mike nodded, sensing danger, or maybe hope.

Snap! Mike had stepped into the trap.

"I want to confess," Chuck looked as if he were attending a funeral.

"Jeeze, did I get the wrong man?" Donovan laughed to divert attention. He knew what was coming and hoped Kat would not laugh at Chuck.

"I love you, Kat."

To Donovan's relief, she smothered him with kisses. "I love you, Chuck. You make me laugh."

"What about you, Mr Donovan?" Millie leaned towards Mike. "Who do you love?"

Donovan stared out the window and sat silently. Dealing with women was not his strong suit. Chuck seemed to be better at it.

Irene or Millie, why didn't I have this kind of luck in high school?

"What are you going to do now?" Millie finally broke the silence, trying not to frown in disappointment.

"How would you like to take the morning train to Guelph tomorrow?" Mike found the courage. "Webster wants my report. I could show you the sights, and I know a great place for Chinese."

"I don't know about the sights of Guelph. Is the Speed River still there?" Millie smiled. "I'll be ready."

Mike blushed. He remembered what his grandmother had said just after he had joined the Mounties, 'When you find the right girl, and she doesn't even have to be good or Catholic, slap them cuffs on her quick. Don't let her get away.'

Donovan looked at Millie and straightened his tie.

"I'm getting a fresh case and better make it good. I spent a lot of the railway's money here and because there won't be a trial they don't think I did much. A conductor has gone missing west of Owen Sound."

"I love Owen Sound," Millie sighed.

"I could show you the sights up there too," Donovan sipped Millie's wine. "I'll be going this week. There's something fishy at Crossing Creek."